DIASPORIC
VIETNAMESE
ARTISTS
NETWORK

DVAN FOUNDERS

ISABELLE THUY PELAUD
AND
VIET THANH NGUYEN

CONSTELLATIONS OF EVE

ABBIGAIL NGUYEN ROSEWOOD

TEXAS TECH UNIVERSITY PRESS

This book is typeset in EB Garamond. The paper used in this book meets the minimum requirements of ANSI/NISO Z39.48-1992 (R1997). ♾

Designed by Hannah Gaskamp
Cover illustration by Moonassi

Library of Congress Cataloging-in-Publication Data

Names: Rosewood, Abbigail Nguyen, 1990– author. Title: Constellations of Eve / Abbigail Nguyen Rosewood. Description: Lubbock: Texas Tech University Press, 2022. | Series: Diasporic Vietnamese Artists Network | Summary: "An intimate portrait of one woman's battles against her own destructive impulses in love, her obsession with her art, and the envy that poisons her most treasured friendship"— Provided by publisher.

Identifiers: LCCN 2021038292 (print) | LCCN 2021038293 (ebook) | ISBN 978-1-68283-137-3 (cloth) | ISBN 978-1-68283-138-0 (ebook)

Subjects: LCSH: Self-destructive behavior—Fiction. | LCGFT: Psychological fiction. | Novels.

Classification: LCC PS3618.O844215 C66 2022 (print) | LCC PS3618.O844215 (ebook) |

DDC 813/.6—dc23/eng/20211123
LC record available at https://lccn.loc.gov/2021038292

LC ebook record available at https://lccn.loc.gov/2021038293

Printed in the United States of America
22 23 24 25 26 27 28 29 30/ 9 8 7 6 5 4 3 2 1

Texas Tech University Press
Box 41037
Lubbock, Texas 79409-1037 USA
800.832.4042
ttup@ttu.edu
www.ttupress.org

For T.S.

CONTENTS

The Cards' Waltz — 3

CARD ONE
The Mute Sculpture — 9

CARD TWO
The Soft Shackle — 119

CARD THREE
Being Eve — 187

The Void of Cards — 205

Acknowledgments — 209

CONSTELLATIONS
OF EVE

THE CARDS' WALTZ

To fling the body into an expanse of blue wasn't about dispelling grief, but about preserving joy. Eve needed to jump before the upcoming minutes, days, months began their demolishing of an entire life that had been so carefully built, every decision made to prioritize love—her family—her husband, her son. And it had yielded unspeakable rewards.

When Eve looked up to check where she was, reality having left her body, she saw a bridge—as though the universe were speaking to her.

She left her car keys in the ignition and climbed the stairs in a daze. Leaning over the bridge railing, Eve deliberated. She didn't want to be another survivor of grief; what for, when up till now her life had been so beautiful, even more than this horizon of retreating sun glow, various blues gaining in space and depth. And more infinite. If she jumped now, there might be time yet for her soul to join theirs. *Why allow me to know such happiness?* She wondered if happiness existed solely so that tragedy could strike more precisely.

There had been many ordinary days, as all good days tended to be. Compared to their friends, they had seemed the lucky ones, the type who needed to be comforted and knew to cherish the person who brought them that comfort, for there resides in people both urges, to love those who tend to our needs and to destroy them for the same reason. It seems foolish for anyone to accept in us what we despise in ourselves, and so wiser to resent them. Yet they had been happy fools. There were things Eve and Liam had both surrendered to achieve tranquility, but it was easy to give up petty desires, dreams of the spotlight that wouldn't be possible if everything else wasn't flooded in darkness. She had been certain that they had it figured out, had understood precisely how to navigate their marriage. Perhaps it was easy to become cocksure about the rest of life when one had love.

That night, she had offered to drive, since Liam had had a few drinks. Blue was in the back seat, chirping about his friend's birthday party they'd just left. As usual, her husband was the one to respond to their son's endless observations and inquiries. Eve wasn't listening—in fact, she'd heard nothing. Their conversations were fading echoes, lifetimes away. She loved them the way one loved the heaven's dark descent, its stars and planets burning on their last memories of light. What a trick the sky was, for even the deepest blue wasn't black, and perhaps even the most assured happiness wasn't whole. Eve thought about other versions of themselves in another life, another universe where the constellations were slightly off-kilter, at once familiar and out of reach. She felt sure, as one was sure of hunger, that she'd met and loved them in another time and space and would continue to do so throughout all eternities.

She couldn't remember exactly how the car had veered off course, its toppling through a grove of trees down a small hill. Why was it that one could never recall the exact details of the event that was the cause of one's deepest despair? And yet events don't let us go, they return, return again, causing us to break out in a cold sweat. When Eve woke from the crash, she didn't need to look—one could always feel when something happened to the people one most loved, definitive and final, when all of life's meaning suddenly drained from the universe. Eve would have given everything to never have known such bliss if it meant not having to face its annihilation.

It no longer mattered if a God or a rearrangement of some invisible symmetries had simply decided that a family had completed its journey. She was ready to join them.

Someone was hurrying on the bridge toward Eve. A woman. She was oddly dressed, her clothes patched in vibrant fabrics, her shoes too large for her frame, her hair full of wildflowers. Had she come to save Eve?

"Don't!" The woman shouted, her arms reaching out. "Talk to me, please. What's your name? I'm Pari—"

Hi Pari, Eve said, or perhaps she'd only thought it as she was plummeting, her soul leaping ahead, crashing into a blue-like calm. A windless day.

On her way down, Eve pleaded to no one: *Please let me try again. Let me meet them once more. Another life, another way.*

Eve was wrong when she thought souls were made of glass, reflective shards cutting the body and taking residence. Souls were echoes that galloped from one cosmic time to the next, bridging the past and present, masked as déjà vus and dreams, disturbing the body about the possibility of lives it could have had—another room to wake up in, another pair of eyes to caress rays of morning light, another way to rearrange life's fortunes and dodge its fatal mistakes.

As many times as it takes, I will get it right.

The woman gasped and ran to the spot where Eve had fallen. She looked down and took out a deck of cards from her bag. They were the only inheritance she had managed to keep: her grandfather's reinvention of the original tarot, all meticulously handpainted. He'd been working on them for most of his life, and towards the end, the images seemed to have bled from his own mind, further and further away from the original. The cards had helped her survive on the street by bullshitting people, forcing readings, and predicting futures they didn't ask for. They were her only treasure. She shuffled the deck, picked three, and without seeing what she'd drawn she tossed them in the water after Eve. The cards fluttered around each other, in a dance, in a soundless waltz. The woman breathed one last prayer for this stranger she had not managed to save. *May your last wish be fulfilled.*

THE MUTE
SCULPTURE

The real had to die for them to achieve a lie they could live with. Liam lay on his back on the lawn and used his shins to lift Blue against a white sky. *Airplane.* Eve tried to look at her son through the pupils of her husband's eyes—expanding circles of steel blue, Liam's gaze matching Blue's perfectly. That narrow space between them, chin to chin, lash to lash, was locked, dense with conspiracy, secrets, and the exasperating loyalty of fathers and sons. They will both betray her. Liam already had and Blue would too in his own way, his singular way of administering pain. He was armed for it the moment he staked his claim inside her body.

The time had come for Liam to begin to forget why and how he had fallen in love with Eve, for his heart to slow to a dull question as he threaded through the rooms of their house, the life they had filled with framed photographs and handwritten notes. Blue, had he been old enough to understand, would have chosen his father even though Liam never would have asked him to pick a side. And Eve would feel grateful for that unbreakable bond between them because that was what mothers wanted, always wanted: for their children to love their father, even if it meant there was little left for themselves.

They were surviving the first heartache. In love, there is no such thing as a minor betrayal. There is bliss and then there is death. Eve crossed the yard with her eyes closed, wondering if by not looking she could undo it all—the first time she'd looked at Liam's bare thighs, that faint smell of salt and blood, that bitter and exhilarating male vigor overflowing his pores that at first had repulsed her and then one day, like a cat searching for the trail home, clasped her to him. Unlike the others, it was his body she'd fallen in love with before she understood what that particular composite of cells meant: six-foot-seven, a height that meant a gaze that hovered above earthly things, a gaze that scanned the horizon for something else, something better. She knew he had found her features pleasing, her adolescent-like body a perverse and wonderful trick, a way to fulfill an animal longing, to delay death.

He felt that they shouldn't have had Blue. *I love him, of course, he is mine,* he'd said after the boy's birth, letting Eve know how necessary possession was to love.

Her gaze froze on the shapes of them, father and son—sculpted into that landscape under the too bright blue sky, a few inches above the layers of disintegrating worms, grass, tree roots. She would keep them there with mud and fire and clay and paint. As fixed as a picture, there they would stay.

If Eve had known how things would turn out, she might have agreed they shouldn't have had children, but then what would they have moved toward? She couldn't comprehend those couples that didn't need change. After nine years together, her body began to crave accidents, a kind of shock. It sought out ways to damage itself, ruthless in its quest. Or maybe it was her mind that couldn't get used to happiness.

"Will the sun rise tomorrow, Daddy?" Blue asked his father. He lay by Liam's side, this creature of theirs, as though sprouted from the earth. Grass covered his ears and temples, framing his face.

"Yes, always, Blue."

"Are you sure?"

Liam paused then said, "No, I guess I'm not sure."

Something stirred in Eve's chest. Her husband always considered his words honestly, preferring not to lie to their child. When she asked him if a dress or a necklace looked good on her, he wouldn't hesitate to say no, and that was why she found it easy to trust him. But it was a mistake to assume that because he was willing to dispense minor pains meant that he'd be just as free with those that were harder to bear, the sort that ended marriage.

"The sun will always rise, Blue. You can count on it," Eve chimed in. She was better at dispensing the little lies.

Suddenly, Liam put Blue down and stood up, seemingly tired of the game.

"I'm going for a walk," Liam said.

"With Blue?" Eve asked.

He hesitated before answering, "Yes, with Blue."

"Don't let him get too close to the lake. He doesn't—" She started to say, but Liam had already turned toward twilight, the other part of the sky.

When Liam came back from his walk, he said, "I'm going to the city tomorrow." It was he who had wanted to move to the country. She had followed, thinking that it made sense to return to his birthplace, and the words sounded beautiful in his mouth: *For the stars. We can see them at night.* She acquiesced to this simplicity. Since they moved, he would return to the city more and more often, sometimes just for the day, but lately, at night too, no matter that he wouldn't be able to see the stars.

In their bedroom, he went over to the dresser and removed stack after stack of clothing, stuffing it in a duffel bag.

"Will you be gone long?" Eve asked, trying to steady her voice.

He grabbed her shoulders without looking at her, without showing her the terrible sadness in his eyes. He pulled her into his arms, his words hot against the nape of her neck. "I don't know how long, Eve. I don't know. I only know that right now I'm packing and then . . . and then I'll get in the car. I haven't thought beyond that."

Eve walked out of the bedroom, down the hallway to her studio. There she dipped her hand in water before jabbing her thumb into a lump of clay, drilling a hole with her nail. She sat down on the stool and worked it, shaped and reshaped until her fingers were numb. Red mud bled into the lines on her palms, dried and cracked as she closed her hands into fists.

◆

Eve wasn't a good mother. She was negligent and easily bored. She didn't revel in Blue's innocent questions, *When is sky? Does orange like Blue? Are all colors people too, like me? Where is Orange?* Constantly, she ached to get back to her drawing table only to find herself loosely holding a piece of charcoal while staring at different sections of emptiness in the room until her eyes blurred. Liam hadn't wanted a child, yet he became the quintessential father, patient as a god, better at the art of entertaining than a circus performer.

When Blue turned three, Eve panicked, having read in a science magazine that statistically, married men tend to have affairs when their children turned seven, the age when children could fend for themselves if left alone in the wilderness. The father was again free to roam far, to look for other fertile lands. They were arrogant to think they were above their instincts.

"How old were you when your father left your mother?" Eve asked.

"Seven," he said. "But his affairs began way before that."

They had four more years.

Eve felt sure that she would lose him.

"If you need me—call if you really need me," Liam said before turning out of the driveway. She resisted the urge to cry, hearing the kindness in his voice, the kindness of a helpful stranger. She stood in the cloud of dust the car left behind, smiling at his absence as though he hadn't really left, that he was playing hide and seek with her like he would with Blue. She kept smiling for as long as she could, until the muscles on her face ached, until her feigned amusement contorted into a grimace. She called for Blue. Like father, like son; he refused to answer her.

Blue. Blue. Eve followed the echo of her own voice to the kitchen cupboard, behind doors, under the bed. *You are so good at not being seen.* She walked outside, beyond the lawn, beyond the field, into the trees. They could still play this game without Liam. Night was descending, the stars not yet visible—a dark plummet of nothing. She tried not to make a sound.

◆

One lonely night in college. A universal night for all young women, girls really, seeking answers to impossible questions: *What is right for me? Who do I want to be?* Feeling like everything they wanted could be found in the flesh of another's body—an end to all ends, where both questions and answers were buried.

Like many others, Eve had been too afraid, too timid to think herself an artist, registering instead for Economics. Her drawings, sculptures, and other attempts were tucked neatly under her dorm's bed.

Best friends by proximity, her roommate Pari and Eve put on the smallest pieces of clothing they could find. Pari wore ripped shorts and a bubblegum-colored t-shirt she'd had since middle school. Even under the dorm's hard fluorescence, her skin looked poreless and as creamy as cake icing. She stood in front of the full-length mirror, swaying to a silent song.

"Here." Eve handed Pari a perfume she'd recently bought, scented like caramelized sugar and distilled orange.

Pari spritzed a little on her wrist. "I could devour myself. I'm a campfire dessert." She laughed, handing the glass bottle back to Eve. "You use some too."

"No; it's for you."

As Eve occupied herself with looking for an outfit, mists of perfume sprayed at her hair, her arms, her legs. Pari laughed. Eve pinched her nose; the smell was overwhelming, sickly sweet. In front of the oval mirror, their images merged, their voices each other's echo—a two-headed creature painted and perfumed.

Eve chose a long, fitted skirt and a short tank that sat above her belly button, which she believed was her best feature, though Pari said it was her nipples that she envied. Eve told Pari that she adored her face—her thick charcoal lashes against pale green eyes (the blessing of her mixed Indian and Scottish heritage), her succulent lips, darkly pigmented even without makeup—and she meant all of it. Eve was proud of Pari's beauty.

A final touch—to announce to the world that they were inseparable—the girls wore matching white sneakers, which they cleaned spotless with alcohol-soaked cotton balls.

The two of them, a snapshot of carnal desire.

Such was the confused power of youth.

That night, on his first try, a nineteen-year-old boy, a year older than Eve was, filled her with enough of his inconsequential fluids to transform into a consequence inside her. The boy had on blue lipstick, leaving a trail of prints from behind her ears, down her belly button to her inner thighs—his lip imprints like moth wings. He kissed her elbows, her knees, her calluses, parts that no one ever paid attention to again. It was a lucky way to lose your virginity, she later learned. Such tenderness takes men years to acquire, and some never do.

She toyed not so seriously with the idea of keeping the baby. In her dorm bed, she lay with her feet up on the wall, digging her toe under a corner of a poster, and dreaming of what it would be like to never be alone again. "My baby and I," Eve told Pari, "would walk on sand and bathe in seawater. We would need no one else." Laughing, Pari telephoned the hospital and booked Eve's appointment.

They went to the abortion clinic together. Eve wished she had felt something, but there was nothing except a slow and persistent sleepiness. The smiling doctor, his latex fingers on her groin, *The Godfather*'s theme song on repeat in her headphones (a nurse had told her the day before to prepare a soundtrack), white dunes wafting under closed eyelids. She knew she was sufficiently drugged when the doctor told her, *It will feel a little cold*, as he was inserting metal clamps in her, but it did not. For as long as she could, she tried clinging to consciousness, but just as soon as she drifted off, she awakened again to one nurse's gentle hand on her shoulder while another pulled her pants on for her. *We gave you a pad because there will be bleeding.* Eve thought suddenly of the rubber duck print on her underwear and wished that she had not worn something so childish.

"Thanks," she said, but still she could not feel, the body too efficient at absorbing shock. Memory, its oceanic depth, was dispersed over different areas of the brain in ripples—intermittent flashes of pain materializing over the years and at the most inopportune moment, without cause—a perpetual melancholia. *Move on, move on*, the body demanded. A walking corpse designed for survival.

This, Eve remembered: Pari chewing gum and reading her biology textbook in the reception area when Eve came out, blood drenched between her legs.

"I'm starving," Pari said. "Want to get fried chicken?"

Eve moved toward her roommate. Underneath her, the waiting room carpet throbbed with every step. She smiled, grateful for her friend's indifference. How much she'd wanted to see Pari doing nothing at all except waiting, but even the most significant events could only thwart human boredom for a little while. Eve didn't cry for that baby until nearly five years later—sitting on the toilet at Liam's apartment, peering down at her toes, and dreaming suddenly about having a child with him. Tears like ice picks. She wiped them away as quickly as she could, embarrassed by a pain that took too long to arrive. On her phone she searched for the blue-lipped boy. He'd become a chef in Colorado. He had daughters. Eve didn't want to live in Colorado, so she told herself she'd made the right choice. Except there was no such thing, no right or wrong when it came to forming or demolishing the possibility of a soul.

♦

While Liam was in the city, Eve contemplated contacting Pari. She didn't live far, after all, having left the city too and settling across the river. Eve dialed. Hung up. Redialed. Hung up again. Their friendship had hardened years ago. A fossilized silence. Eve knew Pari was the one she would go to if she were bankrupt—money being something tangible Pari could give and Eve could take. Otherwise, they didn't know how to be for each other.

Blue played with Dog, both as docile and still as a picture. In her head she named all the things they had: they had Blue, they had Dog, they had a studio for Eve and a garden for Liam, they had a hand-stitched lampshade his mother gave them, they had nights made brilliant by stars. And still the unease refused to be muted or tamed by life's extravagance. She wondered if they had less, would their disquiet then make peace with itself, having been given a definition, a name to hide in.

The hours were stretched and fuzzy. Eve kept her cell phone in her back pocket in case Liam wanted to send her a kissing smiley face or an exclamation point, so displaced and yet perfect in its narrow and circular nature, to let her know he was thinking of her. The last time she received one was nine months and eleven days ago.

It was past noon, so she guessed he had already been in the city for two hours. She bent down to dig a hole in the wet earth with her fingers. Blue watched her. Together they placed the cell phone in its grave, sprinkled some dirt on top. She found a stone to place over the small dirt mound. She didn't have to look at the phone's mute black screen anymore.

Light parted over the grass, splitting the land into half shadow, half blinding whiteness. Eve picked Blue up and crossed the lawn toward the lake. Dog followed behind them, his ears sloped forward as usual, fearful and cautious. Since they adopted him, even after five years of gentle reassurances they still hadn't been able to quiet his uncontrollable tremor, brought on by, as the vet told them, an overly sensitive nervous system making him hyperaware of danger, sensing threats where there were none. Eve often made excuses for Dog when he tore up newspapers, destroyed furniture, gnawed a spot on his hind leg until he bled. *Trauma*, she'd told Liam, *we don't know what his life was like before*. He disapproved. *Don't get attached to the story you tell yourself.*

Unlike Dog, Blue lunged into the unknown as if the whole world was a bed made of clouds. Eve skirted the water, leaned into her and Blue's reflections on the lake's surface. Their faces—their eyes, hair, chins—melted together. Her own childish urge to touch the water, Blue's rippling face. Over thirty years old, she still never learned to swim. Dog had his instincts, but who would save Blue and Eve if Liam weren't there?

"Blue, you have to learn to float," she said to her son.

There was no one else, no mental safety net. Before Liam, in every relationship she'd been in she was always aware of other men, a constellation of possibilities in case something failed. When they married, she'd ended all such contacts. She wanted—to be thoroughly in love, thoroughly lonely.

She forgot how to survive without him.

There was the lake.

◆

When she was twenty-two, Eve had an art show in Florence. All her paintings were sold in the first three days. At night, she walked from one ornate water fountain to the next, buzzed on success. In her tote, always—a small bottle of red wine, cigarettes, several drawing pads. Everything she wanted was within reach. She was alone, but her mind hummed with praises, magazine reviews, predictions of future fame. At one in the morning, the empty cobblestoned street was filled with people she imagined were clapping for her. She tumbled on the steps of a cathedral and fell asleep.

Night after night, she would tumble. Different cathedrals, different men, unprotected sex, trusting the earth would spin the way she willed it to. Under the domed ceiling, under its painted gods and gilded monsters, she sat on a wooden bench before the cross, intoxicated, lips full of a nonbeliever's prayers, her hands cupping her sins, her only offering.

They would meet the year after. She wondered: If she had known she would eventually find Liam, would she have sent more work to more galleries? Drank more wine? Perhaps fucked more foreign men? Although Liam never asked her to give up anything for him, he didn't encourage it either. Perhaps he'd forgotten that she had led him to discover something in himself and assumed that such epiphany was personal, affecting only himself, requiring nothing from her afterward. It was an easy assumption, one many would make—their aspirations were theirs alone, to find, to keep, and to fight for. Over and over again, history tells stories of the dutiful partner, the unquestioning sibling, Tolstoy's wife, Van Gogh's brother, those who stood in the shadow of the gifted one. We all take it for granted that these supportive people didn't want anything of their own. They didn't tell you about ambition—that it could be kissed away.

Liam confessed how he felt about her as though it were a crime: *I'm sorry*, he began, then, *I'm in love with you.* Eve hadn't understood the note of regret at the back of his tongue.

Eve thought about that apology often—its primordial tone—using it as a kind of justification for the way things turned out. How had he known? Maybe it was a common secret that all who loved were doomed.

♦

In the dorm shower, Eve marveled at Pari's new tattoo, the ink a burgundy red made to look like henna. Her whole right breast was covered—her nipple the center of a rotating kaleidoscope, a hypnotic web that spun faster the longer Eve tried to focus her eyes. After their first year in college, Pari had become more exotic, growing her hair past her waist and letting it fall in a thick rush that made her body look like it was submerged in black oil. On her already brown legs she rubbed in a palmful of tanning lotion, a way to emphasize her Indian half. When they met, Pari had spoken with a Valley girl accent and listened to top 40 pop songs. Now her room smelled like clay and incense.

From the beginning, Eve had been afraid Liam would fall for her friend. A part of her couldn't shake the idea that she was only a cosmic necessity to the inevitability of Liam and Pari. She tried for as long as she could to prevent such collision, though the more she observed them separately, the more convinced she became that she was an obstruction to what would be a great love, the kind history would remember and celebrate.

Her happiness was thieved. Her guilt seared into her.

But then what was the name for how she felt about Liam? It'd made her cowardly and fearful. Every word, every action was calculated. How easy he was in their relationship, how exhausted she was in trying to clutch at sand.

Liam thought their meeting was accidental. Eve first saw him on a crisp morning; the air felt brittle. He was on a run. He was the most beautiful man she'd ever seen. She was on her way to class, and fortunately it looked like Liam was heading in the direction of her college. Idiotically, she started to run behind him, pretending to be another student late for class. Eventually she pushed past the stream of people and got ahead of him.

All day, she couldn't concentrate on her lessons, instead devising plans for what she'd do when she saw him again. She needed to figure out his schedule—everyone had fixed patterns, automatic tracks that revealed more about them than their most buried secret. For weeks, she paced the neighborhood's streets, lingered under its lamps, its bridge. No sight of him. She worried that maybe that morning run was out of the ordinary for him and decided to skip her evening classes so she could be a more vigilant watcher. Night after night, she waited, standing under the damp bridge, its underbelly rumbling with the sound of traffic. The echoes of her own footsteps.

For hours, Eve had nothing to look at but the carefree graffiti on cement, powdered blue cursive telling her to *fuck off* and no company except for the occasional yellow-throated thrush that landed in a puddle to wet its beak. She would have gone on waiting indefinitely—steadfast in the belief that her desire was enough to will him onto her path.

Friday night at seven, she spotted his blue shorts and sneakers, the same as the day she first saw him, as he turned the street corner. Quickly she prepared herself.

She'd watched hours of clips of modern dancers falling backward while their choreographer yelled that they needed to abandon the fear of smashing their heads on the floor and *just fall*. In her carpeted bedroom, Eve had practiced along. Now, the concrete beneath her felt unyielding. She sweated so much that she could smell herself and for a split second thought she would give up her plan.

But as the man she'd been waiting for came closer into focus, Eve's ankles twisted out of their places and her legs crumbled under her weight, delivering a performance she never thought she was capable of. Time slowed. She felt her head thud on the ground before it actually did, so the physical pain was less of a surprise.

He ran to her aid. The sound of his footsteps striking the concrete echoed Eve's own heartbeats.

Up close, Liam was *more, much more* than she'd thought. All his features gathered perfectly at the center of his nose. His eyes, gentle and fierce. She knew then that no matter how much she drew and painted, her art couldn't measure up to the reality in front of her. She couldn't help but smile at him. Liam fumbled in his pocket, looking for his cell phone so he could call an ambulance.

"I saw you faint. You just—fainted." A look of concern on Liam's face.

"Nothing hurts," Eve said and meant it. She'd never felt more triumphant.

"You might be in shock. Should I call an ambulance? Can I take you to the hospital?"

"No," she said decisively and saw surprise flit across his face.

"Can I take you home then? Do you live around here?" Looking at her legs, Liam said softly, "You can't walk. Let me carry you."

Like many men, Liam had the savior instinct. Eve nodded and pretended the fall had given her a concussion and confused her enough to make her forget her address.

♦

Liam would tell this story many times while his friends stood around them, nodding with approval, the women nursing a tinge of envy. Sometimes he would tell it to Eve as though she wasn't there, as though they both had disappeared into the myth. He couldn't quite believe how lucky they were.

"For four days, you couldn't remember where you lived, but you refused to be taken to the hospital," he said. "You were so stubborn." Perhaps a part of Liam doubted their story, its flawless serendipity. But stronger than his doubt was the wish to believe that all astonishing things began this way—intangibly, inexplicably—and the more he repeated the story and watched his listeners react, the more anchored their fable was in reality.

◆

The truth was, she'd immediately noticed that Liam had a girl-friend. Her hair ties were everywhere: on the bathroom sink, by the bed, in the kitchen cupboard, all with reddish blond strands twisted around them. Luckily, they didn't live together. She called him that night, asked to come by, but like all men sucked into a mystery, he didn't want to share it. *Not today*, he'd told her. *Someone needs my help.*

Eve couldn't have been happier during those first few days together. Liam had little furniture: a round laminated table, two mismatched metal chairs, and the twin bed where she spent most of her time. His walls were less bare, covered with both prints and originals. In the evenings, he would sit at the table, his hands lit by a circle of light that poured in from the window above the kitchen sink. While tinkering with a circuit board, he would talk to her in short bursts of fragmented sentences as though he'd already expected her to complete his thoughts.

Outside, it was fall. The air hadn't completely abandoned the summer heat yet, but now and then a gust of wind would hiss its way through all the apartment's crevices. Under Liam's duvet, she shivered and sweated. She was content to say little, the pain in her head like an echo that fed itself, each ringing louder than the one before.

Liam brought her juice and tea, indulged her random craving for a different cuisine every night. She wondered when he would ask her to leave. Perhaps he wouldn't. Perhaps he too had been waiting for something imposing, something that materialized from thin air and left him no choice.

She learned that he repaired photography and video equipment. He hadn't gone to college and thought himself lucky to have found a career where his technical knowledge mattered more than a degree. He spoke with a slight inflection of both self-aggrandizement and self-deprecation in his voice. He begrudged students like Eve, whom he imagined looked down on him.

"Emily," Liam explained, "isn't like most people. We get along." She was his girlfriend, and like him she'd ended her education after high school.

"I'm not much of a student either," she said, thinking it was what he wanted to hear.

"But you should be. You already know what you're good at, so just focus on that." His tone seemed to scold.

She began to scratch the skin around her fingernails, ripping out small shreds until she bled. She didn't yet know how to please him.

At night, Liam spread newspapers on the wooden floor and lay down by the foot of the refrigerator.

"Do you want a pillow?" Eve asked, sitting in bed.

"There's only one. You use it."

"You're enjoying this, aren't you?" she joked.

"A little." He turned his back to her.

The sounds of cars passing and music blaring—a jumble of lives outside Liam's window. Inside, they were silent, listening to the occasional click of the radiator. A little while passed before he spoke.

"It's like camping," he said.

"What is?" Eve said to the ceiling.

"You can't sleep because the ground is uneven and hard. You're not used to your muscles and bones scraping against tiny rocks, but somehow you're happy."

She heard him chuckle in the dark. She smiled.

"The only difference is that there are no stars," he said.

"Close your eyes," Eve said. "There they are—thousands of stars, a thousand tiny pinpricks of light."

A little while later, without knowing if she was still awake, Liam said, "How do you do that? Compel a thing to exist with just a fierce belief?"

She would one day ask him if it had worked, if he saw the lights, but not just then.

On the third night, she said to him, "Why don't you enroll at my school? You could take night classes."

He raised his head from another circuit board, put down the screwdriver, "Is that possible?" His voice trembled.

"Sure," she said.

"What would I study?" Like a child, his eyes were wide as though he'd been waiting for this conversation his whole life.

"Anything you want. Math, physics, history, sculpture, anthropology . . ."

Liam went back to his work. His large hands, which usually moved with precision, seemed, for the first time, lost. For the rest of the night, he said nothing. Eve turned to the wall and cursed herself silently for having upset him. She would leave tomorrow, she decided.

For dinner, Liam sautéed broccoli and scrambled eggs. Handing her the plate, he said, "This food might boost your memory." He winked. She laughed.

Dawn had barely broken. The sky was an industrial gray with tangerine veins running across it. Liam left his newspapers on the floor and slid into bed behind Eve. She felt his hardness against her.

Gently, he pulled down her pants. She held her breath. He caressed the crevice from her butt down to between her legs, his breath quickening. She still did not move—afraid that any reaction would unclothe her desire for him, the truth about her fall, the past few days. Underneath Liam she was a flat sheet of paper, without breath. He nibbled on her earlobe and placed a finger between her legs.

"You're wet," he said. With one hand he grabbed her butt cheek and spread it to the side, pushing deeper with his fingers.

"Yes," Eve said.

He freed her legs of her pants and rolled Eve onto her stomach. His gentleness gone. She closed her eyes, pretended to be dead. He disappeared inside her—gasping, she placed her palm on the window glass. Fall was really here. Its coolness cascaded through her.

In the morning, he kissed her.

"How are you?" he said.

Eve nodded.

For years Eve had enjoyed all those loveless relationships, thrived in them. Starting with the blue-lipped boy, even in his slow and merciful way, every man's cum brought her a little closer to death. Their sad dribble in her belly button, their urgent flood on her back, their acid, foul, sweet, clean liquid on her lips, in her hair, in her eyes—her body a graveyard.

The friction, the back-and-forth mechanism and intensity of focus, made her wish for a different kind of beauty, one unburdened with life's continuity. How tragic an orgasm was—an electrified combustion, her first in more than six years of enthusiastic fucking, leaving her slacked in Liam's bed like a corpse. She held her breath, pretended she wasn't alive to rid herself of the guilt of not knowing who Emily was, and of winning over her. The body was a cliché, instantly hypnotized by the object that would indulge its craving.

The madness of her fall, the snapping of her skull on the concrete, days of haunting the streets—all for but a few seconds of white blindness.

◆

One night, Liam said, "My parents loved me too much when I was a kid."

"They are lovely," Eve said. She and Liam had been together for over a year.

"They never imposed anything on me. They respected me, let me make my own choices."

"Is that a problem?" She felt herself getting irritated and tried not to show it.

Liam opened the college's catalogue, smudged the tiny print with his finger. "They gave me no direction. Nobody forced me to take piano lessons, nobody pushed me to make captain of the soccer team even though I was good. I could have been. . . . How am I supposed to know what I'm interested in?" He read the course descriptions out loud, then shook his head.

"If we ever have kids, we'll make sure to give them the right amount of neglect. No respect or love," she said, with more anger than she'd intended.

"Eve." Liam said her name in that biblical way of his, like he was conjuring a spell. She fell into his lap, a docile pet, put the tip of her nose to his. When he closed his eyes, she did the same.

"It's winter," she murmured. "You're outside, pushing a tree trunk through a saw. The more you cut, the more alive the tree becomes—its growth rings diminishing into the heartwood, bruised and fragrant." Eve touched her forehead to his. She had no money, no influence, nothing to give him except for the pictures she painted with her mind.

Despite what some artists claimed, there is a finite number of original inventions a mind is capable of, after which a map of references is formed, making one thing the shadow of another. The same way worn-out travelers arrive at a new destination only to be reminded of a place they have already been. She described to him, as carefully as she could, the alleys of her mind. He inhaled deeply, his love for her something touchable. Eve hid away the pang of spilling, emptying herself of secret treasures. More than anything, she treasured Liam. After a year of standing before a blank canvas, unblinking, unable to see, she threw away her brushes and colors and donated the rest of her supplies.

"Tell me," he begged. "Tell me more."

"Snow falls in big flurries. You can't feel your fingers, so you take off your gloves to make sure of them—your palms dry and cracked. It looks like you've cut yourself. The blood has frozen instantly into the lines of your hand. What you don't know—what you would never know—is that the blood isn't your own. You'd only opened the heart of a tree."

Liam blinked his eyes open, declared, "You're right, I am good with my hands. I should take a woodworking class." He was happy. "And history, too. I want to know how things become what they are."

♦

When did they become who they are?

♦

After Eve put Blue down for his midday nap, the time she'd craved to spend in her studio turned suddenly elastic. She attempted a new drawing, something that didn't remind her of Liam, and drew a line smaller than a mosquito before giving up. Here in the house they had dreamed up together, she didn't know what to do with time. She thought of going to the lake, of learning to float. Such instinct for sinking, denying the lungs air, and returning to absolute silence—

Eve, who,

What did I do to earn such a magnificent deceit?

Eve, how

Liam was gone, but his questions persisted, suspended in the air around their home like fog. She felt her way through the dense white mist, cold minuscule droplets weighing on her lashes, her eyelids. Why couldn't she remember what she did?

♦

Liam's furniture company had been growing at a remarkable rate in the past year. Luxury pieces with five-figure pricing. A few cost more than their whole house.

"We have orders from Germany," he said once. "Germany! The home of perfection, and they're ordering from us."

Eve was glad for him. Although they didn't struggle financially, they remained as frugal as they had been since college.

"All the money needs to go back into the company. We need to plan for expansion," he said. "Do you mind looking at these designs? Let me know what you think of the layout too." He handed her a catalogue.

They both looked at Eve's blank canvas. Washed by a stream of sunlight, the white appeared even whiter and the emptiness even more empty.

"Of course," she said. She thought it was enough to concentrate on Liam's designs, to consider his success her own.

A few years before, when Liam was thirty-eight, perhaps thirty-nine, she was at the showroom with him in the city. He wore corduroy pants, a fitted brown shirt, brown leather shoes. His hair had begun to gray. Watching him, her temples ached, uncomprehending—he was at his most beautiful. The customers, women and men, seemed to hold their breath when talking to him. Some of the men crossed their arms in front of their puffed chests as though wary of a surprise attack. Liam's relaxed composure tended to ruffle the men even more. Perhaps that was why he had more male followers than true friends. Someone came in the store—a well-dressed woman in her fifties, naturally tall and wearing heels. He greeted her by her first name. In jeans and flats, Eve sat down at the counter to avoid being introduced as Liam's wife.

"So, you decided to come back for the table after all," he said to the customer.

The woman smiled, the abashed smile of a teenaged girl. "Oh—I don't know yet. I wanted to see it again." She sat down in front of the live-edge table, instantly frozen into a picture—she and the table both, their statuesque bodies, their candid charms. Liam didn't seem to notice.

He bent down on one knee. "May I?" Before she could answer, he put his hands on her temples, closed his eyes. Too embarrassed to keep looking at him, she followed and shut her eyes. Liam began, "It's winter. You're outside pushing a tree trunk through a saw." The cadence of his voice low to almost a whisper, Eve had to strain to hear. She stared at the room. Her whole body receded into itself, an imperceptible pulse.

The woman bought his table for thirty-nine thousand dollars, brought down from forty thousand.

"A discount just for you," Liam said, and sighed sadly as though it were a true loss.

That evening, his interns opened a cheap bottle of champagne, one of the dozen they had stocked on the office shelf.

"You practically hypnotized her," one said. "You're amazing," they exclaimed in unison. Liam blushed, squeezed Eve's hand, and said to them, "It's just a dream I used to have." Eve never came back to the showroom. She told Liam the smell of wood gave her migraines.

After their visit to Liam's furniture store, she began to paint again. Faces and dream shapes. Whenever Liam asked about them, her throat prickled as though she'd swallowed sand.

"Tell me how you came up with them." He had a towel wrapped around his waist as he sipped coffee from the mug Eve'd had since college. Pari's mug. "I only want to know because I'm interested in you."

"Really?" she said. It was Saturday. Through the kitchen window, she could see a red cardinal pecking at the bird feeder. *Cardinals*, he had told her their name. There were many creatures, plants, topographies in this part of the country that he knew the name of and tried to teach her. Rarely did she remember them. Blue was interested in the names of things too. He would trace his fingers across the landscape and demanded to know. Often Eve couldn't give him the answer. If he insisted, *What is it, Mama?* She would say, "It is what you see." Perhaps this was why he preferred Liam.

Liam feigned hurt, getting up and taking Pari's mug to the porch. Eve poured herself some water and followed him.

"Are you angry?" she asked.

"Wasn't it you who said that all love is, is being interested in something, someone? When you're no longer interested—"

"I was a girl when I said that."

"But you were right," he said.

"Daddy, what's that?" Blue pointed at something in the sky, his voice far and foreign to her ears. A strange bird sound.

Eve looked up, wondering what it was he saw. "Blue, do you mean—"

"That kind of cloud is called cirrus," Liam said. "Blue, do you see how their edges are thin and blade-like, unlike that fluffy one there—cumulus, I think it's called."

♦

After meeting Pari on campus, Eve's mother said, "Don't worship beauty just because you have an eye for it."

"This, coming from you?" Eve grinned to let her know it was a joke. Her mother was a fashion photographer. Her whole life was framed around beautiful objects. Eve was twenty- two years old and in denial of the trajectory her mother had set for her simply by insisting on the importance of the flesh—the ideal shell.

Eve lit a cigarette for her. They sat outside the diner and smoked together.

"I take pictures. It's different. The models are useless without me. I give them context to exist in." She inhaled deeply. "But you. I'm worried about you."

"You're calling me shallow," Eve said, thinking about the blur of fashion weeks, runway shows, beauty pageants her mother had taken her to.

"All artists are shallow, only they justify their addiction to beauty by interpreting it. Rendering it ugly."

"I'm not an artist," Eve said and looked at the sidewalk. Women whisked by, the heels of their shoes clicking on the concrete. Hairless shins, defined calves—she was numbed to cosmopolitan good looks, but she knew her mother was right. She would go on to worship a kind of beauty—so singular it seemed to hold a secret wisdom. She didn't see how it could hurt her.

♦

Their first vacation together in Kyoto, after the wedding—it rained. For days it didn't stop raining.

Eve's father, on his way out of her mother's bed and her life, had left a parting gift: a wooden Japanese puzzle box. There were no instructions, no diagram indicating its final shape, what it was supposed to withhold, conceal. As a child, Eve became obsessed with undoing the pieces, prying and bending them into chaos. She believed that in the guts of the box were her father's last words, an answer to a question she couldn't fully articulate.

She had some preconceived notion that the Japanese were experts at masks, the lineless painted face and the controlled smile, kind and distant, the container of secrets. They stood in the rain, their feet soaked, not knowing where to go. Liam tried to be cheerful, but the silent streets, the meticulously pruned trees, concentric circles carefully traced on sandy beds, emptied him. Liam said, "I feel empty," and smiled as though he welcomed it.

They tried to sleep on the tatami mat, but their feet were cold and their backs ached. When they woke in the morning, Eve found Liam blow-drying her shoes.

"It's raining again," he said. "They'll just get wet as soon as we step out, but you'll have warm feet for a little while."

She had a spontaneous urge then to be honest, to tell Liam the truth about how they met. *Not today*, she told herself, *but one day*. When was it the right time to acknowledge an old lie?

She did not want to leave their heated room, but as diligent travelers they stepped out into the pouring rain. Liam clutched the umbrella as though it were a battle shield. Eve's calves still cramped from their previous days of walking, her toes blistered, her knitted sweater scratching her skin—all the discomfort of adventures burned luxuriously.

It was true what people say: a true desire requires no other.

♦

"Is he Japanese, my father?" Eve asked her mother.

Over the years, Eve had asked similar questions, and received similar non-answers, yet she couldn't help repeating herself, wanting to hear the origin story, or perhaps the lack of one, again and again.

Her mother shook her head repeatedly to show her frustration. "He could have been anything. We only spent one night together. How do you expect me to remember?"

"But you remember he was handsome."

Eve's mother shook her head again, a smile forming on her lips. "You don't forget that kind of beauty."

They were in her mother's living room, languid on her velvet loveseat, once a movie prop—a gift from a director friend. They were sharing a bag of honey-flavored chips, the crowns of their heads touching, their legs dangling on each side of the sofa's arms.

Eve stared at the chandelier on the ceiling. They didn't look like mother and daughter, more like girls.

"Beauty," Eve murmured. There was an excess of it in her mother's staged world. Eve had come to expect it of any room she happened to walk into, curated to enhance effects. She shoved more chips into her already full mouth, her eyes a little teary. How dead all beautiful things were—but she wouldn't have it any other way.

Mother and daughter yearned for the man who had disappeared. The goal of love, Eve was taught, was to vanish the body. More noble to be devoted to an idea, an eternity.

♦

Liam found the folder where Eve kept all the sketches of Pari. By then he and Eve had been living together for two years in the city. After she moved out of the apartment she'd shared with Pari, she still met her weekly and tried to satiate her curiosity about Liam with stories.

"Who is she?" Liam asked, thumbing through the sketches of Pari's profile.

"She's not real," Eve said. "Just someone I imagined."

"Oh," he sighed, almost relieved. "She's breathtaking." He tucked the folder away and pulled her to him. "Your imagination devastates me."

He reached under her skirt, moved her underwear to the side of her crotch, rubbed at her folds until she dripped into his hand. The disembodied orgasm. The estranged pleasure of picturing your worst fear—Liam cradling his hard cock in his palm, coming toward her, pushing his engorged flesh into Eve, into Pari. Her eyes closed. Eve's body sinking slowly into mud, into nightmare. Liam gasped a guttural pain of release.

Liam handed Eve his t-shirt to wipe off the evidence of their fucking. She pressed the shirt between her legs, but she knew the rest of the fluid would come out later, dampening her underwear while she was at work or at the store.

"If I hadn't known she was fictional, I would have thought you were in love with her." He fingered the spine of the Pari folder. Too much of a blessing was a curse. Liam kissed Eve, a mouthful of wonder. She sensed that maybe he didn't believe her. Maybe he would look for her, this dreamed thing, this figment of a girl.

After that, Eve's weekly meetings with Pari dwindled. Eve started to ignore her phone calls, e-mails, desperate and enraged messages. *Tell me what I did. I'll understand. I'll disappear.* Threats and pleas. *I always knew you would do this. I've always had this feeling since we met that I was being extracted—those countless hours of posing for all your art projects. I had this idea that I would be used up, that eventually you would discard me. Then I told myself I was being ridiculous—you were my friend; you were my best friend.* Only after they ceased to be in each other's life did she begin in earnest to draw Pari, more than she ever had. And she couldn't stop. Pari emerged, sketch after sketch, canvas after canvas, chewing on the ends of her hair, walking a dog, standing in a crowd, in a doorless room.

◆

Eve bought a yard of rope, hooks, and nails from a hardware store off campus. The clerk scanned the combination of items, asked, "What's the project?"

"Is that hook strong enough to hang a person from the ceiling?" she said.

"You're joking, right?"

"It's for a friend." Eve grabbed the plastic bag and hurried out before he could stop her.

When she told Pari, she couldn't stop laughing. Together, they looped the rope around their ankles and practiced different types of knots: the running bowline, the soft shackle, the alpine butterfly, the lighterman's hitch. The rope prints snaked across their thighs.

Eve installed the two hooks on the ceiling of their living room. "Are you sure you're okay with this?"

"Who says no to being immortalized?" Pari stood up and pushed the straps of her dress off her shoulders. The dress fell in a satiny bundle around her ankles.

It took a while to weave enough knots along Pari's spine and across her lower back to support her weight.

Surrounded by paper plates, bitten apples, smashed light bulbs from their last party, Pari was held fixed in midair. Eve grabbed her sketchpad and sat down on the couch. She began with Pari's neck, elongated it, wrung it out of position so she looked like a bird that had just been shot, a faint red blushing on its feathers, freefalling from the sky. Eve drew slowly and in sections. At times, she forgot Pari was there. The more her fingernails, her ribs, her thighs materialized, then metamorphosed on the page—her skin feathered—the more indiscernible the woman before Eve became. After a little while, Pari said softly, "I'm in pain." When Eve didn't answer, Pari asked, "Are you almost done?"

"No."

"Could you just take a picture then? Use that as reference."

"You want me to take a picture?" Eve exaggerated her disappointment. "If that's what you want—"

"No," Pari said and bit her lips.

After a few more minutes, there were tears in her eyes. But vanity kept her from crying out, asking to be released. Eve pitied Pari for what she was about to do. Worship was a kind of hate too—

Eve ripped the page from her sketchbook and tore it into tiny squares. The paper snowflakes fell rapidly, like a storm, at her feet.

"What the hell, Eve? What the fuck did you just do?"

"It doesn't look right," she said, pretending to begin anew.

"Let me off."

"Fine." Eve untied her roommate. Suddenly she regretted what she had done. "I'm sorry. I can't force it. We can try again some other time."

Pari landed on her knees on the carpet. Rope markings braided thickly around her body. She crawled to her dress, grabbed it but didn't put it on. She limped to her bedroom and closed the door.

◆

The first hint came as Eve stood looking out the window of her studio. Perhaps Liam didn't think Eve could see him from there. He'd told her he was going to weed the garden. Under the slow burn of the sun, he undressed. In his hands were Eve's sketches— she couldn't make out what was on the pages, but she knew. Liam stroked himself so savagely that Eve turned away and bit her knuckles bloody to keep herself from crying. She didn't know how to be angry. She reached for the trashcan and vomited into it. Liam must have known Pari was real, a touchable being. He must have found her. It was inevitable, this drawing of a circle, the hand pushing the point of a pen forward, closing the gap between two points, an infinite distance.

◆

Night—

◆

After over ten years of silence, Eve contacted Pari. On the phone before Eve could speak, Pari said, "Eve?"

Eve didn't know how to begin the conversation: *I'm sorry I've been keeping my husband from you? Never have I seen a more perfect match?*

"Hey, Pari," she said. "You still have the same phone number."

"How else would you be able to contact me?" Pari said. Eve heard her soft breathing. It was as though she was right beside Eve, her exhalation warming her neck.

"I don't know why I called," she said.

"Why did you?" Then to Eve's silence, Pari continued, "Nobody is capable of losing touch forever. People always come back, don't they?"

Eve told Pari about Blue and Dog. She couldn't bring herself to say Liam's name.

After a little while, Pari asked, "Are you still with the same mystery man?"

"We're married."

"So, it was real. Not just a college fling." Her voice was tinged with sorrow.

"How about you?"

"I've been divorced twice," she said. "No luck in love."

"He's still out there, waiting for you to find him."

Pari chuckled. "You believe in such fairy tales because you live in one. Eve—"

"What?"

"Do you remember when you told me I was the most stunning woman you've ever looked at? You were drunk, but—why did you say that?"

Eve swallowed. "You don't think it's true?"

"I know I'm not half-bad," she said. "But nobody ever . . . nobody ever saw me the way you did. I wish you'd never told me that—"

"Why?" Eve asked, tremulous.

"Afterward, I lived my life based on that *truth*, but it didn't work out at all, Eve. I only realized later it was only your truth."

"I'll make it up to you," Eve said, "I'll—" Her guilt returned. Pari had always had a way of making Eve feel as though she'd wronged her.

"Come over to my house next week. I want to see you," she said. Her tone had changed. "Bring Blue."

◆

Eve's mother's skin smelled of acetic acid. She shifted around in the dark, now and then tilting the stop bath trays as figures clad in sand and seashells materialized on previously blank pages.

"The latent image was already there," she explained. "This only renders it visible to our eyes."

"I know. You've told me a thousand times." Eve played the college student, pretended to be annoyed with her mother, although the darkroom had always been one of her favorite places. Her mother seemed to know this and went on as though speaking about the birth of a photograph were necessary to successfully develop it.

"Here the remaining silver halide gets dissolved, making the image resistant to light. Permanent," she said.

Eve asked why she only took pictures of the exceptionally good-looking, the features so symmetrical they looked alien, the long backs and thin skin where the spines peaked through like running hills.

"Don't you ever want to try something else?" Eve ventured a question that might offend her mother. "It's just . . . you've been photographing models for most of your life now. Isn't it too easy?"

Even in the pitch black, Eve felt her mother's glare on her. "So what if I'm only interested in the surface?" she snapped.

Between them, a thick and viscous quiet. Eve looked at the creatures captured by her mother's gaze. She swallowed. She couldn't deny her mother's skills and experience—the photographs were exceptional—flawless and cold.

"You can judge me, but give it a try yourself and see how hard it is." Her mother held a photo up to the red light. "Try to make people see the soul beyond this beautiful shell. It's nearly impossible. You would have to be blind."

Instinctively, Eve closed her eyes.

Later, Eve found a black-and-white picture of a young man, taken in her mother's bedroom, though it must have been when Eve was a child or before she was born because she didn't recognize him as one of her mother's boyfriends. The man stood with his back to the camera, his head turned to the side. The background was a blur while the man, centered, looked etched on. The side of his mouth turned slightly upward, but the eyes showed no joy, only slightly squinting as though evading light. He looked familiar the way a stranger sometimes does.

"Took you long enough to find it," her mother said from behind. "Who is he?"

"Your father," she said. "A stolen moment before he got away." She took the photo from Eve's hand, fell into her chair, set her cigarette on the ashtray, and studied the image; her movements had the ease born of habit. "He had a quality—something I couldn't identify, but you can see it here, can't you? I didn't know it when I was with him, didn't see it right in front of me. It was something only a photograph could capture. I fell in love with him, but not until I saw this." She picked her cigarette back up.

After she exhaled, for a moment the man in the photograph disappeared underneath a billow of smoke. "I know you think I'm after the obvious, the undeniably gorgeous, but I've been looking for it, what your father had, what I believe only the physically blessed have: a defiance of death, a contradiction to the reality of our world. The curse of being cast with such a spell is that these creatures hover above their own life instead of living it. Everything beyond their own reflection is a total disappointment."

Not long after that day, Eve took Liam to meet her mother. She laughed as she shook his hand as though she had predicted it all: Eve's devotion to the picturesque, her gift to Eve. After Liam left, Eve's mother said, "Play all you want, but don't marry him."

Eve was angry. "Don't talk about him like he's just a shell. He's more than just good looks."

"Yes, he's full of personality from being the best-looking man in any room he walks into." She began to laugh so hard that tears cornered her eyes. "It isn't about him. It's about you. That's the curse of the artist: to be a slave to beauty. I don't want you to have to live a life of surrender, there's still so much—"

"You think being objectified makes you an object."

"Yeah, I do. I've seen it happen enough times."

"I'm not the kind of artist you are."

Eve's mother smiled, a pained and satisfied look on her face. "So finally, you admit it. That you're an artist."

◆

Eve tried to deny that life had an elegant way of repeating itself, that when she saw Liam running that day she was the age her mother had been when she playfully pointed the shutter at Eve's father and took the first photograph without knowing it would dictate the course of her life. She didn't want to be the kind of artist her mother was and told herself never to draw again, perhaps an extreme reaction to her mother's fortune-telling. For a while it was enough to use her imagination to build Liam's dreams—theirs. When you've spent a long time deceiving someone, it is a shock to discover the other's catalogue of lies is even more rigorous and painstaking than your own.

◆

They were driving on a stretch of road where there hadn't been another car for miles. Out of nowhere, Liam exclaimed, "All this is just a construct, Eve, don't you think?" To their left, a cliff dropped off steeply. She looked at the slanted trees and asked him what he meant while her heart jerked in anticipation of where this conversation might lead. It wasn't like him to speak in abstractions.

"I don't know how to put it exactly, but lately I just have this feeling that everything around us is fictional," he said. "We fabricate these ideas, stories, like money or churches, and then we attend to them as if they're God-given."

Eve wondered then if such thoughts were the by-product of becoming a father.

"We're real." She tried to suppress the tremor in her voice. Was their fiction falling apart? Eve tried to count the years they had been together, but suddenly she could not recall. It felt like just yesterday; it felt like a hundred years.

"Eve, I know. But sometimes . . ." he hesitated. "We feel like a story too." He said this in his usual affectionate tone, almost kind.

Eve turned on the radio to dodge responding. Liam rolled down the window, let the car fill with mountain air. Perhaps betrayal begins like this, when you realize how easily one story could be traded for another, the truth a piece of clay that doesn't hold a single shape.

"Eve, I think I'm lost."

"What? You're not lost—"

"Can you look up the directions? I don't know where we are."

Eve typed the destination into her phone as the car continued into the knots of the mountains. She turned around to look at Blue, only a few months old then, strapped in his baby seat. It would take almost nothing to grab the steering wheel then and veer it to the left, plunging toward the real and irrevocable.

♦

Where are you, my son?

Since Liam left, the game had become endless. All day, Eve looked for Blue. She followed the clues—footprints on damp leaves. She treaded lightly, trying not to leave remnants of her presence.

Their playground had expanded beyond her control, farther into the woods, nearer to the horizon. The more she searched, the better Blue hid, camouflaged in nature. She laughed at the thought of him wearing a crown of thorns, his body clad with dried irises. Like Liam, he was stubborn.

She paused at the base of a hemlock tree, having stepped on something hard. Her body's temperature increased as she bent down to pick up pieces of broken clay. She touched the paint residue on the tree trunk; this was where Liam had smashed their sculpture before going to the city.

Why do you intend on leaving me with nothing?

Eve screamed for Blue. A sharp pain flashed in her temples. Dog followed listlessly behind her.

"Help me find him," she demanded of her loyal companion, whose ribcage was more visible than she'd ever seen.

What's wrong with you? What's wrong with you?

She held Blue to her chest, his shoulders stiff, digging into her collarbone.

"Blue, are you asleep?" she whispered. She stepped onto the edge of the lake. The water a biting cold. Dog began to bark, but his voice did not carry, absorbed by the trees and sky.

They couldn't continue this story without Liam.

Eve's mind a soundless, sightless chamber—she couldn't imagine anything beyond what they had.

◆

They chased the dark as though it were a creature to be captured, tamed, diluted with light. Liam turned off the car's headlights and the path seemed to open up, to ease and carry them silently ahead. It felt as though they weren't moving at all. Into the mountains.

"My father has been looking forward to meeting you," he said. She tried not to let him know how afraid she was, of the thin and thorough black, of the words *my father*—so ordinary to him, so utterly unfamiliar to her. She thought it required having had a father to know how to behave in front of one. Eve always assigned fathers the omnipotence of gods. In front of Liam's, she would become transparent, and then he would see that she wasn't good enough for him.

For almost a year, she'd managed to dodge his invitations to bring her home, to meet the other people that mattered to him. Then one day he insisted gravely as though their future together rested upon the others' approval. Liam wanted their validation, their blessing. Eve wished then, selfishly, that Liam were more alone, less whole, so that love could do what it set out to do, what it existed to do: healing and transforming the mundane to the extraordinary. Instead, her love for him was simply a continuation of his personal history, different only in its expressions, ultimately familiar and anticipated.

At the very beginning, during one of those snowstorms that coerce confessions because they have nowhere else to be, she told him that she wasn't good enough for him. The TV was on so Eve nudged closer into his side—it was the first time they were doing nothing together.

"Hm?" Liam said, his eyes half-closed, as he was falling asleep.

"I'm not good enough," she said.

Whether he didn't hear her or chose not to respond, Eve was grateful. A few minutes later he said, "I'm so glad we're stuck here together." They had only been together for two months.

Even in the dim light of the driveway, she could see that like Liam, his father was handsome. He was tall, shoulders slightly hunched forward, broad and slender at the same time. His hair, blond streaked with gray, was tied back. Eve smiled to herself, thinking about how well Liam would age. His father kissed Liam on both cheeks and then kissed Eve's left.

"Hello," she said, her neck as stiff as the handle of a hammer. Liam and his father fell easily into a conversation about the weather, an item on the news, the broken heating pipe Liam would help him fix. She walked behind, following in their shadows.

In the kitchen, something was cooking on the stove. Various vegetables were spread out on the counter. Liam grabbed a knife and an onion and began chopping it. Eve panicked without a task but didn't offer to help because she was afraid of making herself too familiar. She leaned against the counter to watch Liam and his father move around each other gracefully in that narrow space. The refrigerator was old and hummed loudly. Liam's father handed her a bottle of wine to open. She was both glad to have something to do, but also worried that she would drop the bottle on the ground or break the cork so half of it would be stuck inside the neck of the bottle. Her hands trembled, her palms moist. It looked as though her fear had manifested into reality; the cork broke. Eve looked at the two men helplessly. Liam's father eyes seemed full of pity for her, as though asking Liam, *This is who you've brought home?*

While they ate, Liam's father told them about a dilapidated house up the hill—a new source of excitement for him and his men at the fire station. The house was scheduled to be burned down in three weeks.

"We can walk up there later. I'll show you," Liam said.

"It's a well-known family dispute around here," Liam's father explained to Eve. "The Moreno siblings have been fighting over that house for a long time. It's been empty since I was a boy."

"Better burned than lost," Liam said. A few years later they would move in next door. Now and then a strong wind would pick up the ashes of what was left of the Morenos' house—from their window, they would watch slivers of ash drift by, sometimes mistaking them for snow.

Upstairs in Liam's childhood bedroom, Eve picked at the corner of a peeling poster of a basketball player. As a sixteen-year-old teenager, he'd graffitied the walls: fireworks of dark blue and rusty red, though the spray paint had faded for the most part. He pulled her close, kissed her cheeks and neck. Seeing her among his memorabilia had made him more affectionate. They moved to the dresser by his bed. He opened the first drawer, pulled out a deck of baseball cards, shuffled through them, and tossed them back inside. From the second drawer, he took out a few birthday cards from his friends in high school, people he was still close to; ticket stubs, pictures of past girlfriends, letters and declarations of love.

Eve lay down on the rainforest-birds comforter and looked for an empty space on the ceiling. She found one in the farthest corner where a spider hung from its thread. Liam pushed her pants down to her ankles without warning. They both knew she wasn't aroused, but still she opened herself, pulled him in with both her legs. The spider had nestled inside its web. He got on top of her, thrust vigorously, their pubic hair chafing against each other. She closed her eyes and thought about tomorrow when she would reach up to the corner of the wall with a wet rag and wipe away the spider and its web. There might be room then, for her.

Liam was fast asleep. She was thirsty, so got up and went downstairs. There was the sound of mice scurrying around in the dark. From the kitchen, Eve could see, through the porch screen, Liam's father sitting on the stoop. She poured herself a glass of water from the sink and walked outside. He must have thought it was

Liam approaching because he hurriedly put out his cigarette and threw the stub in a thorn bush.

"Sorry—I—" Liam's father said.

"It's me." Eve sat down next to him.

"Oh. Could you not tell . . . you know. I'm trying to quit."

Eve nodded. Liam's father took out another cigarette from his jacket's pocket and lit it, asking her at the same time, "Okay if I smoke?"

She assured him it was. She wondered when she would stand up for something, but the sentiment died as soon as it appeared. She stayed until he finished smoking and went back to bed. It seemed no matter where she went, she was a devoted witness, her eyes unblinking as wisps of smoke dissolved into nothing at all.

◆

Eve needed to remake the sculpture. *Wait for me, Blue. Just a little longer, I'll find you.* The clay felt warm, almost human. Perhaps the last one simply wasn't convincing enough. Perhaps Liam would return for this. She pinched the sculpture's toes, smoothed and rounded their tips. She remembered the first time she held Blue's foot in her hand and marveled at his long second toe, so much like Liam's. She bit her bottom lip. How agonizingly difficult to replicate something so simple. Her wrists couldn't relax, infecting the sculpture with their stiffness. Dog whimpered at her feet. He was hungry. Eve forgot the last time she had eaten; she'd stopped counting the days since Liam left.

"I'll feed you when I finish," she told Dog. No man deserves a canine loyalty. She should have kicked him, made him leave. But he was patient, waiting for Eve to return just as she waited for Liam.

Outside, the weather was turning. The first snowflake. Or was it ash.

♦

Blue had a fever. He demanded that Eve turn on all the lights in the house, even the one in the basement. He was worried that if the house wasn't flooded with light, Liam wouldn't be able to find them. Liam had been gone for two nights. She told Blue that his father was working in a city so electrified that it would illuminate his way back home. But she didn't have Liam's power to convince—Blue immediately asked in that honest, heartbreaking way of his, *What if light didn't cast only light, what if they cast shadow, varnishing dark upon dark?*

To please him, Eve lit candles in an already bright room, covered the floor with flickering lights. Still, scraps of night bled through the floorboards, the ceilings, the walls. This boy of theirs was so sequestered he no longer believed in other people, other lives. Beyond the pines, oaks, and cedar, he believed. . . there was no beyond, only his mother waiting for his father to come home from the no-beyond.

"Close your eyes. You need sleep or you won't get better," she told her son.

His eyes stayed open, unblinking. Eve placed her fingers on his lids, gently pushing them closed, but the pupils remained hard, searching for more light.

Hadn't they wanted exactly this for their son? To grow him with the sun and grass, the songs of birds? Now Eve was afraid of how little human contact he had. He and Dog would spend entire days together, getting into blueberry bushes, sniffing at flowers.

52

Soundlessly they moved through the terrain with a confidence she'd not managed even after learning to identify the natural threats, Blue always barefoot. His longing for Liam steadfast and singular—this son of hers, too much of hers.

Eve lay in bed with Blue, the air on their chests, his tiny one and hers, the heat from the nape of his neck, under his arms, in his belly, curled and uncurled, coalesced with her own cool. When he finally fell asleep, Eve crept from one candle flame to another. In the fire's shadow flickered the silhouette of a man: *Is that you? Have you come back to us?* The moment her voice mired the air, the figure melted away.

She blew out the candles and went out to retrieve her phone from under the stone. There was a voicemail from Liam: *Hi Eve, the interns and I had breakfast this morning at the diner you and I used to go to. . . . Do you know which one I'm talking about? It was where we first talked about starting a furniture company. I didn't think I could do it, but your ambition for us, for me, was unyielding. Thank you.* Despite herself, she smiled. How long could they be sustained on their gratitude for the past? The familial love a cursed thing, memory lasting too long, holding them captive in the no-beyond.

She sent him a message: *I remember our diner*, and then because she couldn't help returning to the present, *Blue has a fever and is asleep.* She filled him with details about her day, the little of it, to avoid asking, *Where are you sleeping tonight? Where have you been the last two nights?*

◆

We ask questions knowing the answer would be untruthful. Still, we ask because we need to be lied to; we need help to deceive ourselves. The perpetuation of a fiction is always a mutual effort.

Days turned into weeks. Liam had been gone for nearly three weeks. He asked her again on the phone if she was fine on her own. He didn't ask about Blue, his rising fever. Eve said yes with false cheer in her voice, grateful that he still respected her enough to play this game of choice, pretend her answer mattered.

"I'll drop everything and be there," he said. "If you really need me. Just say the word."

"We're fine," she said. The leaves had turned gold and begun to fall. She'd neglected the garden Liam scrupulously tended to. Rows of overripe onions rotted underground. "We eat an onion a day." She added this lie for no particular reason. "Blue loves to—"

"Please, Eve," he interrupted. "I can't hear about Blue anymore. Not like that. Tell me something else."

"But he—"

"Please."

Eve wondered if Liam still loved them. She worried if he saw the state of the garden, he might leave for good. She'd grown accustomed to this ache—Liam's slow departure, transmuting her panic into hope. As long as he didn't explain, as long as they spoke only of events orbiting his absence but not of the absence itself, as long as—he could still return.

Suddenly he mentioned what neither of them had for weeks: "Why don't you come down? Take the Honda." Eve's old car, the one she'd had since college, the wheels overgrown with grass. A mocking reminder that their distance was physical, could be fused.

"I suppose I could," she said. "I just need to clean it up a bit." Briefly, she felt this possibility simultaneously twinkle and extinguish.

They both knew Eve hadn't driven in over ten years, the first thing that faded away after they got together. They had chosen their house based on its proximity to a grocery store an easy bike ride away, to a school for when Blue came of age, the essentials. Even still, she hadn't needed to leave their property in such a long time, using only the rice and pasta they had bought in bulk. The thought of the market, exchanging pleasantries with the cashier clerk, seemed unbearable. It seemed they had unconsciously planned for Blue and Eve to manage without Liam. On the phone, they played with Liam's suggestion until their conversation waned to its natural end.

◆

Pari complained of strep throat. The girls were bundled together on the couch. She'd had a persistent cold since the winter semester started. She sat buried under layers of blankets, randomly pushing buttons on the remote control, not caring what appeared on the screen. Eve offered to make her tea.

"Two cubes of sugar," Pari said.

"And a tablespoon full of honey, I know."

Pari had grown dependent on Eve, on the way she had all her quirks memorized and carefully adhered to them without hesitation. Eve didn't question her friend's habits, even the ones that would be considered unhealthy. If Pari wanted a smoke, Eve lit her a cigarette knowing it would only worsen her throat. Perhaps it was blindness. Or cowardice. Eve believe that she only wished her friend well, but how was anyone sure of their intention?

That extra spoon of honey that made it sickly sweet, undrinkable to anyone else, would have been trivial, forgotten if not for the following morning at the diner with Liam. Eve watched him add two sugar cubes in his cup, stir, then wave the waitress over to ask for honey.

"Sugar and honey?" she asked, thinking of the only other person she knew who did the same.

Liam squeezed the plastic bear bottle until the sticky fluid almost dripped off the side of the spoon. "This is how I've always liked it. I don't even like sweets normally, but for tea, there's no other way."

"Why don't you try adding just one or the other next time?"

"I have. It just doesn't taste right."

She nodded and added the same to her own tea, which she usually took without sweetener. But for the rest of the morning, she couldn't bring it to her lips. She already knew what it would taste like.

The sooner you learn that the person you love will be in bed with someone else the better, Eve's mother said like a mantra. Eve knew it was to justify her inability to stay with any one man for long, but the brain often implemented these falsehoods as defenses against suffering and death. Always death. They were crusaders for immortality, persisting in their search of lesser pains.

Eve wished to share Liam's memory of their weekend mornings at the diner, in which they accidentally said things that the other would remember forever. But she couldn't recall the details except for their changing outfits according to the seasons, which were perhaps more inventions than memory, and her ears ringing with the sound of ceramic against metal as Liam stirred honey into the already too sweet tea. Was she in love with him then? Or had she wanted him with the simple agony of a child wanting an ice cream cone, at all cost, that she didn't even question if it was right? She wasn't the first to have looked at him, yet she was convinced that she was the first to have discovered his singularity. *Unfortunately*, Eve imagined her mother say, *the stone had more ownership over the miner than the other way around.*

If Eve had allowed Liam to meet Pari, would the three of them have become better people, people whose life pieces opened up like a solved puzzle box? The cruelty of the almost perfect marriage was just that—for a while, Liam was content not to look elsewhere. She hadn't made him miserable; she had made him happy enough. Eve wanted to tell Pari about Liam as she had about the others, to invite her participation in the conquests, the joy that wasn't true joy, the despair performed and tears shed that were more for her eyes than for whichever man she'd been with. Pari continued to ravage her body, drinking more alcohol than water daily, fucking men who repulsed her, snorting cocaine in dim hotel rooms—all for their shared giggles, faithful to the story she and Eve had created together. And as Eve laughed with her, pretended she'd done the same while her gaze was toward the end where the road cut off, where the land slid into a newfound abyss.

In the club's bathroom, Pari took off her underwear, examined the mucus of white discharge on her triangle lace.

"Fuck," she breathed. "Another infection." She held it out to show Eve. The other women grimaced and exited, swinging the bathroom door.

"That doesn't look good. Maybe we should go home," Eve suggested, less for Pari's sake than her own. Eve had decided to be loyal to Liam—there was a first for everything. But even as she said these words, she sprinkled white powder on the back of her hands and inhaled it clean. Pari slapped Eve's head affectionately.

"I'll go with you if you need to paint," Pari said. "Not for anything else."

Eve shook her head. She didn't understand her friend's insistence on her pursuing art as a career. Pari was more serious about that than her own studies. Though Eve's mother liked to think

Eve was following in her footsteps, it was Pari who had convinced her to switch majors in her second year of college, and again it was Pari who pushed her to apply for fellowships in Italy where she would eventually have her first exhibit.

The girls danced, accepted the drinks strangers brought to their lips, pretended they didn't notice the circle of men closing in. They weren't drunk but knew how to act the part, loose limbs, slurred speech, holding eye contact a little too long, too intensely, and then turning sideway as though offended. The worse their behavior, the thicker the circle grew until they were pressed together, ribs to ribs, crotch to crotch, mouth to ear—the nucleus of catastrophe—their life reduced to sensations, rhythms, the urge to fuck. There was no better happiness. Everything else was impossible: *Why the classes and lessons? Why the arduous pursuit? Why art? Why relationships? Why marriage? Why job? Why children? Why wake up?*

Why?

It was then, the hatching of a thought, infantile in the way a child hounded whys until the adult had to turn to the stars for answers. Maybe it wasn't so much the hatching as the return of something always felt. But Eve didn't know it yet, not that night, having misread an existential nothing for inspiration. They returned to their apartment with two other twenty-something boys trailing behind them. As they walked, Eve could feel her resolve to be faithful to Liam melt away, overtaken by the more immediate impulse to please Pari.

In the living room, Pari rolled her tights off her legs, examined the fresh bruises on her thighs and knees.

"How did this happen?" she said.

Everyone marveled at the purple blotches on her legs. Eve considered inviting Liam over and watching him fall in love with her roommate. Maybe she was drunk, but she didn't feel afraid—Eve was Pari; Pari was Eve. One didn't exist without the other. Pari grabbed the phone from Eve's hand, saying, "No drunk texting."

"I wasn't—," she said. But she'd lost the will.

The two boys looked at them and then at each other, probably trying to figure out the logistics, probably asking themselves if their lust was enough to overcome the embarrassment of being naked together. They were a version of Eve and Pari and for that, the girls wanted to punish them. They drank more, swishing vodka over their gums. They talked. The boys learned that Pari studied biology, an undergraduate and already a research grant under her belt, and Eve sketched. The more the boys knew about them, the more their hearts swelled, their intention transformed, their penises shrank. Pari and Eve were a long-term quest; they would have to find somebody else to screw—for tonight falling asleep would have to do.

When the boys realized this, they passed out immediately, drained. Pari went into her room, came out clutching permanent markers of various colors. Eve picked the orange one, commenced drawing barbed wire on one boy's wrist. Pari joined her with the traditional black, sketching out a game of tic-tac-toe on the boy's forehead. They giggled nervously as they stepped around the bodies, hovered their feet over the boys' heads, afraid they would wake up, afraid and excited of the potential violence of their anger.

Eve drew and drew, hearts and stars and crosses, the most elementary and the most sublime. She loved drawing in that moment; her fingers burned with the passion of endings. And when she was the last one awake—Pari had fallen asleep between the boys—Eve drew on her too. As soon as the pen's tip touched Pari's skin, Eve felt sick, as though she were vandalizing a coffin, her own body, but she couldn't stop. Whole pictures emerged. She filled them in with colors. She stayed up until her eyes felt blind and then—as a final declaration—she wrote in block letters across Pari's chest I HATE YOU. Would that do it then? Were they finished? Eve left the apartment, left Pari alone with the strangers, took a taxi to Liam's place. She couldn't breathe; her own chest felt scorched with the words she'd left on Pari's.

Liam opened the door; it was four in the morning.

"You're not wearing shoes," he said and took her in. He wrapped a blanket around her.

"I'm sorry," he said. Eve muttered nonsense in response, though she didn't understand why he was apologizing.

"I'm sorry," he repeated, "But I'm in love with you." He gave her a cup of tea, made the way he liked with two sugars and honey, told her to drink it. "You came to the right place."

Betrayal—it seemed to Eve then—necessary to love.

♦

Together, she and Liam rediscovered the city, ecstatic to smell the metallic, smog-filled air, ecstatic to drink whole bottles of exquisite wine followed by cheap Chinese takeout that made their stomachs ache. They exulted in their firsts of everything: walking down the aisles of bodegas, being late to their appointments because they needed a little more of each other after making love, inventing their own language to describe a state of feelings they believed had granted them access to a new reality. They pitied their family and friends. They celebrated small pieces of luck with zealous devotion. Events, people, objects had aligned for their convenience and pleasure—they found themselves incredibly lucky to catch the subway right before it left the station, and if they missed it, they would sit on a bench and kiss, devouring each other in an infinite embrace, and laughed when they again missed the next train. They asked themselves, *Who were we before?*

They sat on Liam's windowsill and smoked until the joint was a nub, barely pinchable between their fingers, then Liam leaned over and kissed her. Their tongues curled and coiled, a fusion of the familiar and unknown. Eve's mind flipped through pages of thoughts, scene by scene, sensation by sensation. How they ended up on the bed, she didn't know.

Afterward, he held her head in the nook of his arm, said, "I wish I knew you when you were a girl; I would have loved you then too."

Eve pushed her face into his armpit, held the hair between her teeth and pulled. He squirmed and pressed her even closer to him. Licked her cheeks. He knew it would make her laugh. For a second, she closed her eyes. Rain. Metals collided. She stared into large white lights.

"What's wrong?" he said.

Gone—Liam's body, crooked smile, lovely face. Love was not of the body. Nights like these tricked Eve into thinking they were eternal. She felt like tears.

"I just imagined you," she said. "I saw that you were dead." Only death could defeat them, she felt. She pictured it often, her fear sending a shudder down her spine.

"I would gladly walk off a cliff to make you happy," he said.

Like everyone who believed they found the reason for life, for existence, they misunderstood the people they became together as who they had always been. *I know you, I know you,* he whispered with such severity that Eve trusted it too. She decided that she also knew Liam, that she understood him thoroughly.

♦

Blue and Eve were above the clouds. They stood at the top of the hill, overlooking other hills, other trees. From there, she could see Pari's house, its white walls, its open windows without blinds, a life proudly on display. Could they be friends again? After all these years? Eve closed her eyes; Pari came into her mind as vividly as she was standing there.

"I never graduated college," she told Blue without quite knowing why.

He didn't respond, more interested in the blackberry bushes, pricking the tip of his thumb with their thorns. "I met your father and decided that he was more important than the rest of my life." What was it about mountaintops that solicited confessions?

"Blue, I want you to meet my friend."

"Friend?" he said.

"In college, I used to have many friends. I used to go to parties where there would be a lot of people," she said. "I was a different person, maybe. Or, perhaps it's that I loved someone else, *something else*, before your father."

"Really?" He perked up, now interested.

"Yes. I had a close friend," she said. "Her name is Pari."

"Is she dead?" He plucked a handful of berries and gave some to Dog.

"No, why would you ask that?"

"Because you never see her. When things die, we don't see them anymore," Blue said.

She realized he was remembering something Liam had read to him. It was a story intended to teach children about impermanence.

"One pari, two paries, three . . ." He counted each berry.

It shouldn't be so easy to say a word, speak a name when it had been dormant for so long, but it was. She knelt down and helped Blue pluck more berries. "Four paries, five . . ." they said in unison. The relief she felt.

She dressed Blue in his favorite blue overalls. It was apparent that he was a gorgeous boy and he'd already mastered that grating stare as though to unclothe your soul. He did this, long blond eyelashes unblinking, as he looked up at Pari and as she swayed awkwardly at the door of her home, unable to break his gaze. Mutual admiration on their faces and the faint red hue of blood rising in Pari's neck.

"Hello," Pari said.

"Hello," Eve said.

"You look good—well, like you," she said. Eve appreciated this small kindness. Glancing at Blue, Pari added, "I'm glad you're still an artist."

"You look the same." Eve smiled. Pari hadn't changed, though maybe she'd become less flashy, more elegant. Her maroon lipstick matched her dress. Glass earrings of birds shone against her jet-black hair.

Blue ran inside, thrilled at the empty large spaces, high ceilings, polished tile floors, so different from their own house of small corners and wooden floors. He disappeared up the spiral stairs. "Careful," she warned him. Inside, their footsteps echoed.

"Do you live here . . . all this space—" Eve began to ask.

"Alone, yes," Pari said. "I get this house, he the ones in California and Florence."

"I'm sorry—"

"It's not my first divorce," Pari said, as though this were a point of consolation. "Tea?"

Eve declined. "Wine?" she suggested.

Pari laughed, going to the kitchen and pouring two glasses of red. "God, I've missed you."

Eve sat down on an armchair, kicked off her shoes. Pari didn't look. It was as though they both found it perfectly normal that she was there. It was then Eve noticed her friend's side table, Liam's signature design.

"Nice table," Eve said.

"Oh, yeah, German design or something."

"Have you ever been to the store?" Eve asked. "In the city?" She remembered Liam's hands over the customer's temples.

Pari didn't answer, as if she'd already grown bored of the topic. "Blue—did you name him that because . . ."

"Yes."

"Does your husband know?"

"No." She smiled.

"You're wicked," Pari said. "To wear your secrets on your sleeve like that. What if he finds out?"

"He won't," Eve said.

The women laughed, and in instant, they were girls again.

"That's what I've been missing, maybe—the right kind of secrets," Pari said. "My exes both knew too much about me, all there was to know. I would tell them the most mundane things on my mind. Confess my sins on a regular basis. I didn't hold anything back. I'm beginning to think that maybe marriages require more restraint."

"Did you tell them about me, then?"

"No."

"Not all there was to know, then."

It was never easy between them, but it had always been fun.

They finished another glass of wine, then another. While Pari got together a plate of snacks in the kitchen, Eve went upstairs to check on Blue. He sat next to an open chest full of new toys. It looked like he'd opened several brand-new boxes. She bent down to pick up the pieces. "Blue, you weren't supposed to—these aren't yours." She was about to scold him when she noticed, hanging on the wall at the end of the hallway, the torn-up sketch she'd done of Pari in college, her body half-human/half-bird, suspended in mid-air. The drawing had been carefully taped together and framed.

Pari came up the stairs. "Who are you talking to?"

"You never had kids?" Eve said, still looking at the picture.

"Never could." She said this without sadness.

"Why did you keep that?" she pointed.

"I really thought you'd be famous by now," Pari said. "And, I don't know, nobody saw me the way you did. Nobody looked at me, really looked, with as much attention. It's sad, I know, but I didn't expect you to ever be here to see the drawing again."

"Neither did I."

Eve thought about the folder she had at home. She thought about telling her friend that she didn't need to look when she could see Pari with her eyes closed.

"Do you still draw?" Pari said.

Eve nodded. "Sometimes, but I—it doesn't matter—I'm not ambitious."

"It's such a waste," she said. "Not everyone is so lucky to have such a gift, and when you do, you should use it. It's your responsibility."

Eve laughed at this, more loudly than she'd meant to. Liam had often told her the same thing, the very same words.

Eve, do something with these drawings. Why don't you let anyone see them?

You see them.

Not just me. People.

Perhaps what he meant to say was, *Why are you happy being nobody?* Perhaps he was uncomfortable with the idea of being with someone so unaccomplished.

"Why is it so wrong to devote your life to someone else?" She said to Pari what she had never said to Liam. "I don't find art useful, worth sacrificing your family for. I don't—" She couldn't control the tremor in her voice or pull back the tears from her eyes.

"Eve, I'm just saying—" Pari was ruthless. "I just think you should have more. You're not meant to be some housewife in the country. The sculpture you made is: *more* than real. Better. That's how good you are. Isn't that what art is—you've told me once— more than life? Or do you not believe that anymore? But if you're happy. . . . I'm sorry, Eve. I am."

Eve wondered what sculpture Pari was talking about, but she was getting too heated to ask. "And what do you do, with your gift?" she snarled.

"What? What gift?"

Eve gestured to Pari's face, her hair, her body. "I suppose you use it. I suppose it gets you what you need."

Instead of yelling at Eve or telling her to get out as she hoped Pari would, she lowered her voice, said calmly, "I don't know what it is you see with your warped vision, Eve. I'm ordinary. I have always been. When we were in school, when people approached us, you would say it was because of me. I thought you were only trying to make me feel good, not that you actually believed it. You must know that it was because of the two of us together. We complemented each other. We stood out in a crowd because we were together. We were young, we were girls in skirts, that's all. It was fun while it lasted. Like I said, I wish I'd never listened to you. Maybe then I could have made the right decisions for me. After you left, things changed."

Without Pari, people stopped seeing Eve, but that was to be expected. She now hated Pari's false modesty more than she'd ever hated her good looks. "Do I really have to try to convince you of how fucking beautiful you are? Do you know why you've never met—" Maybe this was where Pari had wanted to lead the conversation after all. Eve had almost said too much, let slip that her whole life had been shaped around a fear.

Pari sighed. "Do you want another glass of wine?"

Eve nodded.

♦

Five weeks since Liam had left for the city. His phone calls were brief, but just as tender as ever. She explained to Blue that when someone was absorbed with work, he might forget about other people.

"It's a blessing," she said. "You'll see when you're older that not many things can hold you spellbound so completely that everything else around it dissolves."

Blue closed his eyes while she spoke, as if he were shielding himself against another adult justification, another adult lie. How could she prove to this son of theirs that undivided attention was the fundamental mechanism underlying all the world's greatest inventions and that it was rare and called for sacrifice, when Blue was so easily captivated by everything he saw, smelled, touched. Before Liam called, Eve always prepared herself for a fight, thinking of all the anger and derision she couldn't restrain, but even over the static connection, the warmth of his voice soothed and quieted her. She didn't ask when he would come home, and he didn't say.

Her routine adapted to Liam's absence and filled it with her walking toward and away from Pari's white house, its white windows and door trim. For the first time since Blue was born, she began to leave him and Dog alone. Pari worked as a biochemical researcher at the local university, so they would meet nearby for dinner and drinks. But always they would find themselves back at her large, empty house where their whispers were a cold and distinct echo. They shared the snowy white velvet couch, the cushions too tightly packed to be comfortable, but they didn't notice because their lips were wine-stained, their bodies slacked and warm. Relieved to be together again. No reason left for Eve to resist her instinct now. Her mother had once told her that it isn't the muse itself that inspires the artist, but the power struggle between them.

Their movements were stirred and pulled by the strings of shared memories. They followed this remembering like happy puppets. One night, Pari pulled a Ziploc bag of dried shrooms from her purse. She spread them on a gold china plate and poured a bag of trail mix on top. Eve laughed. How could she say no to this woman? She scooped up a handful and tossed back her head as though she wasn't a mother, a wife, as though she was nobody at all.

"Yum." She coughed. The tart sweetness of the raisins and M&M chocolate couldn't fully mask the moldy plant. Pari smiled, taking off her heels. When she sat down, her silver dress rose to above her knees. The faint shape of her body appeared and disappeared under the silk as she moved.

"Will you be my friend again?" Pari asked.

Eve had forgotten how hallucinogens burst language open, leaving splinters on the tongue, intentions unable to distill into words. Pari seemed entirely unaffected by the drug. For the first time, Eve saw something else, something other than her beauty: a pressing sadness, an urgent void that deepened with each passing second. It haloed around Pari, emerald and white. Was this what she meant when she insisted she was ordinary? Eve looked down at her own arms to see if this light outlined her too.

"Yes, yes, I'll be your friend forever," Eve said, her head dizzied with all the promises she'd made, to herself, to Liam, to Blue. The weight of words strained against the odds of life—words would likely lose, yet they continued to write vows, declare their commitments. Her words made her feel invincible. They absolved her of shame—she crawled to Pari, rested her head on her friend's thigh. "I left you alone with those two guys from the club, I didn't care what they might do to you, I stopped speaking to you without any explanation, I didn't contact you when I heard about your miscarriage, I still didn't reach out when you were going through your first divorce, or second," Eve listed her sins. What she didn't manage to say, *All of this, out of adoration.*

"I slept with every guy you dated in college," Pari said.

"Blue-lipstick?"

"Yes, him too."

"Why?"

"I don't know."

Eve didn't know what to say so she screamed as loudly as she could.

She looked at the ceiling, its paint an eggshell white that didn't match the rest of the house. Eve felt the urge to smash something—the sculpture of a child breaking into five identical octagonal pieces. The confessions were fresh, but the crimes were old. She still hadn't told Pari about Liam, her biggest sin, and decided then that she never would. There were others who lived without love and Pari would be one of them.

Pari jerked her leg, startled. Afterward, the air in the room felt even quieter than before. "Are you going to betray me again?" she asked.

"No," Eve said. "I promise."

♦

One day, Eve asked Pari, "Do you still deny that you're very beautiful?"

"There are plenty of women . . ." Pari said.

"They all wanted you. Everyone I was with. You told me yourself," Eve said.

"Men can't help themselves. That is what they do."

"Do you do that now? Sleep with married men?"

She nodded. "Sometimes."

"Who is he? Tell me about the man that is worth wrecking the lives of others for."

Pari looked over her shoulder to make sure no one else was listening, then sighed. "He's—I don't know if you can understand—he's a good match for me. It sounds simplistic, but how many people can you say that about? I've gone through enough men to know."

There it was: the love argument. It was just as flawless as the God argument because it explained everything and justified all. Eve finished her mimosa and ordered another. She found that she still admired in Pari what she would despise in others. When she sucked on long strands of spaghetti, letting red sauce drip down her chin, Eve was charmed. When she tore families apart, she seemed empowered. Her freedom was fearless and without remorse. Between sips of white wine, she spoke of her research, something in biotechnology—Eve wasn't so much listening to her as watching her. In her mind, she was already painting. She would have to use egg yolk, an old-fashioned paint binder, but it didn't dry as quickly and allowed for movement, more shapeshifting.

"When it's ready, I'll test it on myself," she said. Eve didn't ask her what it was she hoped to cure.

"Is it worth it, always doing what you want?" Eve said. Pari's life seemed the opposite of her carefully curated one.

Pari shrugged. "One of the perks being that you don't have to think about it."

"You're a slave to freedom then," Eve joked, but Pari didn't laugh.

They clinked glasses, finished their wine.

♦

Liam had seen Pari once, perhaps more than once, although he didn't know it. The city was big, but they had carved out sections and faithfully followed their patterns. The campus, the bar, their apartment, another bar, the bodega where she bought her cigarettes, his office, sometimes the park. Eve knew only so much was in her control, that she couldn't prevent his private pattern, away from their shared life, from colliding with Pari's. The three of them were in the same neighborhood and going to the same university.

Eve sat and smoked on the college grand steps to wait for Liam's class to end. She always came early. In waiting she found her panic transformed into calm, her fear of losing him into strength. She was the only one waiting so she was the one who deserved him.

She lit another cigarette, inhaled, and released the smoke toward a sky that never darkened. She'd forgotten to bring gloves; the bones in her fingers stiffened against the chill. It was the first day of winter, the transition in temperature so abrupt that it felt like being robbed of a human essence. Liam was ten minutes later than usual, but she couldn't make herself get up and go inside the building to look for him. Her body felt like a statue during an earthquake, shuddering repeatedly yet paralyzed. It was a role she'd unknowingly chosen since the moment she pretended to faint under the bridge, that she would always be the one waiting.

There is only one Origin story, her mother had once said, *the beginning determines everything.* Eve remained on the granite steps for another hour when her phone blinked. Liam told her to come to Enigma, a bar a few blocks from their school, a place she'd been to countless times with Pari but never with him. He didn't apologize for breaking their habits and she refrained from showing her irritation. Years later, when Eve recounted that night with hurt in her voice, Liam said as though perplexed, *But I never asked you to wait for me.*

Eve applied color to her lips before entering the bar, which had already spilled over with people. Groups of college students huddled outside the door. Liam waved at her immediately as though he'd been anticipating this moment his whole life. Such childlike delight was the bedrock of his charisma. She ignored the greetings of a chatty bouncer who had once seen her dragged out of the bar muttering incoherencies.

Liam was in his early thirties, about ten years older than almost everyone around them. The most attractive girls, roused by the confident and stable aroma of a mature man, buzzed and swayed around him. He shied of the fact of being older than Eve's classmates, which made him all the more charming.

One girl, his classmate, told Liam about how much she enjoyed his presentation, adding, "I'm really interested in what you said in class. Would you want to discuss it over coffee sometime?"

He glanced at Eve quickly, then nodded, "Sure."

She drank to stop herself from noticing. Pressed against the bar counter, she was exhausted. He smiled at her, amused. He seemed to realize for the first time that she was a college girl, younger than him, and it pleased him. He bought her more drinks and she tilted her head back time after time.

"I'm having fun. Are you?" Liam asked.

She nodded and felt the sudden urge to urinate. She pushed her way through the hive of bodies to the restroom. The door was unlocked so she opened it, then quickly apologized because someone was already there. The girl had her back to the door; she was standing on top of the toilet's lid and vandalizing the ceiling. Before Eve could leave, the girl jumped down and grabbed Eve's wrist.

"Hey, Pari," she said, knowing it was her as soon as she started to move. This place was after all their most-frequented bar.

"Where have you been?" Pari locked the door behind them. "You just disappeared for weeks after we came home with those guys! I was worried . . ."

Eve chuckled. They weren't the kind of friends who worried about each other. It was more like them to court disaster and weep over the ruins.

Eve tried to change the topic, "So, how was the threesome?"

Pari dismissed her question with a wave. "Where have you been Eve? We're roommates. I'm supposed to know whether or not you're safe." Her language was unfamiliar, as though she was actually crafting each word as she spoke. The light bulb above them blinked in and out, making Pari's face appear over and over again.

"I've been staying with this guy . . ." Eve said and looked to the spot where Pari was writing on the ceiling—a small, dense square:

IhateyouIhateyouIhateyou
IhateyouIhateyouIhateyou
IhateyouIhateyouIhateyou
IhateyouIhateyouIhateyou
IhateyouIhateyouIhateyou

"A boyfriend?" Pari asked.

Eve nodded.

"Is he here? You have to introduce me."

"No, he's not here."

"Okay, fine," she said.

Eve sensed that Pari didn't believe her. She noticed then that her friend's eyes were red and swollen. Eve decided that Pari had probably just smoked so she didn't ask.

"Want to see something?" Pari untucked her top from her jeans and lifted it above her collarbones. Even in her disarray, she was still breathtaking.

"What?" Eve said.

"Look closer."

In between her breasts, in faint white ink, were the block letters Eve had once written there in marker. "Fuck," she breathed. "Pari, what did you do? You got it tattooed?"

Pari turned toward the mirror, traced her fingers over I HATE YOU. "I thought a lot about what you could have meant."

Eve pulled her friend to her, ran her fingers over the permanent words.

"Let's go," Eve said. In that moment, Eve knew she couldn't have both of them in her life, knew she would have to choose.

As Pari and Eve left, she looked back at the bar and caught Liam's gaze. He looked to her right shoulder. His and Pari's eyes met. He tried to move through the crowd toward them. In a panic, she grabbed Pari's hand and pulled her into a run. Outside, gulps of cold air filled her lungs; Eve had forgotten her coat. When they were close to their apartment, Pari asked, "Who was that?" Eve told her that she didn't know, that Liam was just someone she was talking to.

"If you don't want him, I'll take him," Pari scoffed.

"I have a boyfriend," Eve said, ending the interrogation.

Nauseated from the sprint, they tumbled around in the kitchen, managed to find an opened bottle of red wine. When Eve poured it in their glasses, she caught a faint vinegary smell. Pari smiled. The corners of Eve's lips curved upward, mirroring her. Pari leaned on

her as they went out into the hallway and climbed fourteen floors
to the roof. They didn't feel the cold air, their hearts still rapidly
thumping. The air was misty; around them, the city blinked in
and out of the smog. They knew there would be no stars but
looked up anyway and stared intently at the sky as though their
gazes were enough to will a sense of beauty into existence.

"Will you come with me to get it removed?" Pari said, rubbing
her chest.

"The scar would be worse than what you have now."

They leaned over the rusted metal railing. Their bodies pen-
dulumed so far forward that their feet hovered a few inches from
the ground. The thought of falling made them giggle. Eve had an
urge to push her friend over, to destroy her beauty and at once
immortalize it. She wanted to draw Pari, reproduce her image,
multiply her person. Pari stepped back from the edge as though
sensing death, then announced, "Let's come back here in thirty
years. If our lives don't turn out as we hope, we'll jump."

"And what if—what if it turns out exactly as we expected?" Eve
said. "Isn't that just as good a reason as any?"

Eve held the wine glass out over the railing, dropped it. The
space around her shrank, tornadoed inward. She held her breath
as the glass's stem split from its cup, as everything cracked into
earthly shimmering stars.

◆

Liam held up a string of lights connected to a portable battery.
They had hiked for four miles in the snow to arrive at this clearing
of white—a lone pine tree to their left. Eve blinked twice, dark and
light collapsing into a thin line. He told her most of the trees had

been cut in preparation for the holidays, but he had written to the farmer and asked for this one to be spared. She joked that it was like looking into an optometrist's machine when getting your peripheral visual field measured: in the distance always a single red-roofed house. She chattered to keep from being swept into the landscape.

Up close, a ladder leaned against the tree trunk; empty beer cans scattered about, half buried in snow. Liam had been here before, perhaps more than once. He didn't waste time but immediately climbed to the top and unwound the string lights. He whistled a tune she didn't recognize while tossing sections of string onto branches. Eve held the ladder secure and looked at the ground to hide her face, wet with tears. She knew then that his love for her was absolute and that the vast silence, the sky falling into snow forming a perfect convex, would fix them there. Such beauty had nowhere else to go, except toward a diminishing.

"Ready?" he asked.

She was.

Liam flipped the switch and the wild pine tree was dotted with lights. Fireflies transfixed in time. His face in their shadows. He leaned back to admire the completion.

"What do you wish for?" she yelled to him, to the treetop, the night sky.

"To marry you!" Liam said. Words continued to ping pong back and forth between them, though she could no longer hear them. She accepted his offer then—in the history of mankind perhaps an unremarkable gesture, the sense of repetition and yet the acute certainty that *this*, this was unprecedented. She laughed then at the totality of her happiness. She accepted too all future anguish and disappointments. She accepted that such love must and will die.

They couldn't stay long. The hike back would be more difficult at night, the path jagged with rocks. Liam had spent most of his energy planning and getting there so that he slowed to a few paces behind her. She was afraid to look back at the dark shape of him, his moonlit face furrowed with fatigue. She didn't know how to spend the next moment, next day, next year, how to fill them—the hours like a body on life support. The loveliest breaths already taken, the pinnacle already reached.

Eve soon learned that what Liam deemed sacred couldn't also be sensual. Her body failed to arouse him—gone his famished animal gaze on her flesh, a new affection took place. He became almost paternal. She felt herself transformed from lack, her body adopted a perpetual state of longing, her skin a sheet of glass.

The bedroom turned toward shadows cast through the window by their maple tree, and every now and then by the swift, black silhouette of a bird. She lay on the cold sheet and stared at the gray wall that glowed briefly from a silent flapping of wings. She tried to masturbate lying on her back, then on her stomach, on her knees, with half of her upper body dangling off the bed, but a surge of melancholy would come right before the moment of climax, keeping her body from its primal goal. Even her monthly blood became lighter, nearly translucent.

One day, Liam remarked, "You look thin."

Standing on the balcony, Eve felt weightless. The more mass she shed, the thinner her desire became. And she needed it, this lightheadedness, this slow erasure of self. Within the silence, she discovered something better than happiness. She wanted to guard it.

Liam talked more to compensate for Eve's wordlessness, laughed louder to combat the fraught air in their home. In the middle of winter, he heated the house to the point of perspiration. Every night he cooked for them, meals that Eve dabbed at. His gaze pinned on her throat as she swallowed. In his own way, he was trying. She realized too late that marriage was defeated not by a lack of care, but by uncoordinated timing.

At the news about Blue, she felt Liam's relief.

Everything was stalled in preparation for his arrival. They would leave the city for upstate. They would raise him in the country. Neither of them mentioned Eve's thinness, the danger it posed.

♦

Blue came—the wished-for punishment. Before him, Eve had kept children at a distance, seeing in them humanity's ego, a temporary solution to an ancient fear. Against a well-honed, lifelong belief, she wanted him.

♦

They had just seen a film, their third time that month at the cinema. They'd had five peaceful years together and began to envy their friends who always seemed to be in a crisis. They watched movies, discussed fictional lives to satiate their desire for catastrophe. Perhaps it was difficult for anyone to accept a good life once they had it. The film had quieted them; they left the theater in the stupor exceptional art tended to induce. They were awestruck by the possibilities of their lives and pained by the prophesized regret that would come no matter which path they chose, for every decision for something was a decision against something else.

Eve was still high on the film, its labyrinthed structure. She talked and talked, reproducing the story again in banal words, describing scenes from memory as though she were the only one who understood their meaning. Then she said something self-deprecating because in the presence of art that succeeded to be authentic seemingly without any commercial compromise, artists as consumers became suspicious of their own work, unable momentarily to blame their failures on the ignorance of the public.

She complained that because paintings were static, they couldn't compete with moving images, which shuffled emotions, played one feeling against another seamlessly. The story had been possible because of the form. Recalling a moment in the movie, she asked Liam, "Don't you feel overwhelmed by how many options there are?" She illustrated this point clumsily by pointing at the intersection in front of them, the multiple streets they could walk. "And if it's true that even something so trivial as choosing the left or right side of the sidewalk would irretrievably change them, the person who wakes in the morning isn't the same one who goes to bed at night." She said all this lightly, meaning only to entertain him.

"Let's not sleep tonight!" She hopped backward ahead of Liam, feeling as though behind her the buildings, trees, and pavement were melting; sky and electrical poles, garbage and paint bleeding into one another. They were only a few steps away from a different reality. She sought out the street's reflection in Liam's eyes but saw only her own nervous expression.

Liam nodded along solemnly, said without any self-consciousness, "The movie was nothing but pretty propaganda. What choices?"

She blushed. "But we are making choices right now. You can't deny that at every moment, we're presented with—"

He shook his head; blood had risen to his neck, "There are decisions that fix us in a moment forever. Afterward, we don't get to metamorphose; we don't get the privilege to grow or decay with the seasons. There comes a time for a choice that is an end in itself."

Eve smiled, mistaking Liam's flare of anger for affection as she often did during those first few years, believing that love had invented them, that history had been dreamed by an amnesiac, and nothing had preceded what they had, who they were. She wrapped her arm around his waist and agreed hastily, "You're right. This was determined a long time ago."

Perhaps he had wanted her to prove him wrong, to argue that no single act had an all-encompassing power, but she preferred as young lovers did to hear in everything affirmations of their feelings. She didn't know that had she only asked—how close Liam was to the edge of confession.

How many other conversations did they have, one appearing unconnected from the other, as they slowly exposed frayed ends, evidence of their loose grip on the fiction of a life they had authored? Their impending madness, a faint brushstroke on the horizon, always a breath away.

In the dark, he asked, "Are you awake?"

"Hm." She was in that half-conscious state.

"I'm not doing too well in the design classes. I can't figure out the programs, but it's more than that."

"I know, you're so good at it," Eve said, drifting to sleep.

"They're all young and talented, and I'm—late? It seems so foolish of me."

"I know I'm younger than you," Eve yawned, already gone to a different reality. "I don't care about my talents, not as much as your success."

She rolled away, her back to his whispers. Liam placed his hand on her spine, between the shoulder blades. Soon, he, too, fell asleep. The dream hung between them, hypnotic, a misunderstanding.

♦

Was there an isolated moment when they became aware of their unhappiness?

Blue had moved on from playing with plants and sticks to mortar and broken bricks. He liked what was left of the burnt house next door. The exposed wooden columns, tiled floors overgrown with grass, the roof open to the elements. He built whole cities from the charred materials—his only means of communication. He'd stopped speaking entirely. If Liam were there, perhaps he would be upset to find Blue and Eve inside such a dilapidated structure, but even his phone calls had stopped.

Eve and Blue were in the no-beyond, where there was no consequence.

Light, sapphire and diamond-sharp, brushed her closed eyelids. Standing under the ruined roof, she allowed herself this momentary rest, this gentle soak of memory. Some mornings, upon the waking of consciousness, she tried to will her eyes shut a little longer, but always they peeled open to a second-rate reality. The body persisted. It moved from one space to another. It took in air.

She sent Liam a text, asking, *Why is it so important for you to be happy?* She switched her phone off after that because she knew he wouldn't respond. She didn't understand the compulsion to chase happiness. The pain of wanting him had been greater than any joy. She lit a match to warm her hands.

The sudden deprivation of light, shadows stretching their way into the farthest reach of the house, Dog's insistent whimper, Blue's silence—it was as though they were all starved of beauty. She had given up on stoking the fireplace, the outdoors crashing into the indoors, the walls groaning from chill—they were shadows moving upon shadows.

Eve didn't know how long she'd been pressed against the corner of the bathroom when Blue touched her elbow. His gentleness splintered through her. She said, dumbly, "Are you hungry?" as though that was all he needed of her. He shook his head, touched her arm again more urgently than before. They walked to the living room. Blue didn't need to point for Eve to see Dog lying in front of the cold ashes of the fireplace. She put her palm on his belly, rubbed it manically as though her icy fingers could re-summon his warmth. She looked at Blue, who had stayed a few feet behind her, intuitive as all living creatures were to the departure of a soul.

"I'm sorry," she said to an empty room. "I'm so sorry."

Dog's open eyes stared unblinking at her tears. She pushed on his lids that felt like rubber, but they refused to close. She picked up the heavy mass of him, which had stilled into his usual sleeping position, and then—realizing she did not know what to do with the corpse—put it back down.

Eve looked at the clock, something she hadn't done in a while. It was time to cook dinner, so she draped a blanket over Dog and went to work in the kitchen. There sat Dog's empty food and water bowls. She wanted to believe she had given him food, but she couldn't recall exactly when. She cried harder as she moved around the kitchen looking for something edible. She chopped the last of the wilted vegetables into smaller pieces, roasted them, boiled pasta, made a creamy tomato sauce. Blue crept around, now coming closer to her, now further away as though he couldn't decide if he should trust or fear her.

Her hands trembled, and when she spooned the sauce onto a plate, it splashed on the counter, the floor. She meant to pick up a towel to clean up the mess, but instead her hand grabbed the blade of a knife. The shock of the sharp metal against her palm, the splitting of skin and flesh—its paper-thin sound—calmed her, though only briefly. Blood trickled on her clothes, blossomed there. She squeezed her hand in a tight fist, digging her nails into the wound. She thought about the possibilities of her life—its finality. She thought of the lake, of how she wouldn't feel the cold. She thought of taking Blue with her, of not taking him. She pictured holding them both submerged under the calm of lake water and wondered if she had the strength. She thought perhaps she should ask Blue what he wanted.

"Why have you gone silent on me?" she derided her child. "Blue, say something." But he clung stubbornly to his wordlessness.

She exhaled sharply from the release of her grip on their life. What of afterwards? People would come. People always came when it no longer made a difference. They would walk through the rooms, tread lightly as though the house were a museum. They would claim the sorrow as their own, discuss it with hushed reverence as though they were members of a private club. They would talk about how lovely Eve's family was and how perfect; meanwhile, in their hearts, they would blame the mother, always the mother. *How utterly selfish,* they would say, never in their own lives having loved to the point of obliteration. The privacy of the world Eve and Liam had meticulously constructed would crumble as all palaces do, the initial effort too grand to be sustained.

♦

Short bursts of nightmares. Not hers, but Blue's. He recounted his dreams by drawing them, vivid and glowing with green and orange crayons; he was afraid of them, even the good ones. In the childish drawings Eve recognized broken fragments of Liam's childhood, places and objects they had never told Blue about— the marshland, the muddy pond, red cardinals dipping suddenly in low bushes, a silky, wet pavement, Liam's father's missing boot (found later, overgrown with ferns, the heel stuffed with sunflower seeds), someone's index finger balancing a dot of blood.

The boy's eyes seemed to beg, *I want to go there, Mama, take me there*, and she shook her head, *I can't, I can't. It's a place in your head; it doesn't exist.* He'd been crushed then, gone back inside his silence. She'd crushed him. *You understand, don't you? Why I had to.*

So frail were his limbs, so fine the strands of his hair. On the bed, there he was, a hybrid of bird and ghost.

♦

Blue had a feeling that another version of him existed elsewhere, if not one other version, then multiples, and if not one elsewhere, then everywhere. The sky was ruthless, glowing with such intensity that he couldn't bear to look at it. In his backpack were the chess pieces he had stolen from his classroom.

A knight, a queen, and a pawn.

Both the queen and the pawn were white marble, and the knight black. He didn't understand why he was overcome with the desire to separate those three pieces from the others, to rescue them from the crowded board. Blue's heart beat so loudly in his chest that he sang in order to listen to something else, to quiet his guilt. It wasn't that he was afraid he would get caught, since getting caught often came with the most predictable punishment. The consequences of getting away were harder to pinpoint, because every misfortune that happened afterward could be traced, reasoned back to the original crime, and so more painful.

Running away from the crime scene—the school—Blue tripped on a half clamshell, fell and smashed his knees against a smattering of rocks (each one alone too small to do much damage, but together they made him scream). Dots of blood trapped under the skin. He picked up the shell—not a particularly beautiful one, plain white, not yet eroded by the environment. It would reveal its fluorescent purple someday. In his palm, it looked a tiny and ordinary thing. Angry, he tossed it to the side of the dirt path, against a fence. He never paused to think how the shell could have gotten there; the ocean was far away.

But for a moment, an inconsequential moment while he still had the half clamshell in his hand, Blue heard the breaking of waves and assumed the sea was always there, somewhere nearby. Far from it. This was the first wrong thought, a mistake in a series of wrong thoughts to follow. Blue would grow older and older and when his life defeated him as though he was just a pawn in his own game, he would try to backtrack, to see where things had gone so wrong, had ruptured into various combinations of nightmares, but he'd never be able to find his way deep enough into this particular past, to the clamshell—already lost to his memory the minute he threw it away and indiscernible to the rest of the world. It started to rain. In the bushes against the fence, the shell began its long process of erosion.

A dream Blue dreamed.

♦

How could we bring someone into this world just to fill our emptiness? Liam said. The next day he brought home a bouquet of lilacs. The flowers' perfume still reminded Eve of their first lie.

At Liam's apartment, they had sex on the kitchen floor, grimy and thick with oil from years of being sprayed with cooking, Eve on her knees and elbows, back arched, rear spread and splayed open to Liam's ramming and gazing. Fucking like this always made him wild. She wondered who he really saw as he looked at the back of her head: maybe the first *Eve*, the primordial woman. Nothing else, no matter how inventive, could compare to the most basic human instincts—the deepest fantasy. She wasn't on birth control, her body reacted severely against it. Liam knew and came in her as a way of apologizing for the question he'd asked, a way of saying *Fuck it, we can do it too. Have a baby. Everyone else does, so why shouldn't we?* She was grateful for this gesture.

After, they went to the drugstore for Plan B. The fluorescent lights, their merciless white glare, made everything uglier. Liam had paid for the pill once before but didn't offer to this time, so Eve would feel like it was her choice.

At the counter, she felt a sharp ache in her knees. Minor scrapes and cuts that hardly counted as injuries, but always a change in her after their lovemaking. A dimming as evening light rendering more and more transparent. Liam stayed the same throughout the years, always larger than Eve, more relaxed, more savage, as though sex fed him, deepened his masculinity. Eve kept thinking about her knees and looked down to check. Dots of blood underneath the skin.

All the while, Liam talked about how the city urged and oppressed them. "Let's go somewhere this weekend. Get away," he suggested. The pharmacist nodded along as though she were the one he invited. Humans had a way of blaming the environment for their private turmoil. Eve agreed that it would be good for them.

"Let's get away," she echoed him.

Out on the street, standing next to a discarded mattress, a smattering of tiny holes from cigarette burns on its surface, she swallowed the pill with a gulp of water. She didn't feel her insides rearrange, didn't feel the silent working of the pill dissolving, its various chemicals like soldiers at war against uncertainty.

♦

Nobody warned her of the intense ache she would feel in her mid-twenties, the dogged endless inner dialogue—if she deserved to be a mother, if she deserved not to be a mother. Other women, the more blessed women who followed their instincts and did not wrestle with the question of whether they loved humanity enough to perpetuate it and the thousand questions that followed, dismissed Eve's anguish with a wave of their hands, *You'll know, you'll feel it when it's time*, as though feeling was enough justification for doing. This type exasperated her, but worse were those convinced of humanity's ills or who were past their biological prime and would try to impress her with anecdotes of miserable parents, monstrous children, environmental disasters, so relentless were their convictions that they would not let go until you declared your membership to their club. She envied everybody who had made a choice. To decide one way or another seemed to her as arrogant as declaring the existence or nonexistence of God.

She envied and resented Liam for being able to stay in that quasi-agnostic state of the desire for reproduction, time not being as much a physical determinant. *Why toss the dice again?* he'd said. They were lucky people, satisfied with nearly all aspects of their life; something was bound to go wrong with their child.

What he didn't say was that their unit of two was only an idea, uninvincible, unguarded against random violence, chance, their lives exactly what they were—a die midair waiting to land. Love had made them arrogant.

Even with their frequent weekend trips to Liam's father's upstate farm, Eve thought the city would last them forever. They relied on its industrial misery, its collective loneliness, and always its rude waking—like so many other artists there, she bartended and waitressed, her hours dusty, smoke-filled, vermouth sweet. The throb in her heels, her lower back a testament, she thought, to her commitment to beauty, to art, though she wasn't painting, not then. She took care that her fingernails and toenails were always polished, spending considerable time applying on them minuscule star and moon glitters. Because of them, she was well tipped. Sometimes it occurred to her that she could pay her college debts quicker if she sold her body.

She read hundreds of accounts online, anecdotes from other broke female college students, many with master's degrees. One claimed that she got her hymen sewn back together, pretended to be an underage girl, and auctioned off her second virginity; it was enough to pay off all her loans. It didn't help that schools had become increasingly politically neutral, that students were corrected on their linguistic misusage of "prostitutes" as opposed to "sex workers." Eve was confused by her own attitude, worrying that not taking advantage of the opportunity of a high-paying gig meant she was prejudiced, sexually unliberated.

Too many times, customers would brush the back of her thighs with their pinky fingers, subtlety enough that it could still be deemed accidental. Once, on a slow night at the restaurant, at a table in the back garden, a man had pulled her to him while she was taking his order. She ignored him and continued to read the items out loud: a Stella, a chicken sandwich, a side of sweet potato fries, the type of order she'd received a thousand times before and a thousand times more since, a meal any ordinary man—a professor, a laborer, a father—might have placed. Sensing her lack of resistance, the man became emboldened.

"You get this a lot?" he asked.

She nodded.

"Why, do you think?"

"Because I'm a waitress?"

The man had lain his entire hand on the back of her leg. Without warning, he grabbed the thin triangle of her underwear and slipped his fingers inside her. Eve gasped. She did not move. She didn't understand why she couldn't step back like she normally would have, laugh off the customer's advances, and count the tips later. Curiosity, perhaps.

The city opened doors of darkness under the guise of intellectual tolerance. Eve entered its chambers one by one, came out adorning slime and pus as personal trophies. She didn't know yet how angry she was at what the social conscience demanded of her, at how little substance her sense of self was composed of. And because of this, she unfairly exalted Liam, turned their love into worship as all lost souls do.

Eve was nearing the last semester at her university. Just when the college lessons—the historical and theoretical, the theological and scientific—began to accumulate thickly enough for her to form semi-educated thoughts of her own, her body responded with a fierce *fuck you*, opting instead to produce midday hallucinations of her various future selves, a recurring fantasy of rape, the ultimate nullification of choice.

She imagined the shadow of a man, his will engulfing her body. The roll of a die. She imagined telling Liam that she was taken by surprise, that she'd had no choice.

Twenty-six years old, Eve began to take night walks, skirting the river at the emptiest hours, long after twilight. She hesitated at dark corners, shuddered from a combination of excitement and fear. She followed hooded figures and lingered in their shadows until abruptly they turned their eyes to her blank face. "Can I help you?" the gentleman among them would ask, and she would retreat, relieved she'd not been split apart, her body still intact.

When she got home, they made love cautiously, Liam withholding moments before cumming to put on a condom. Suddenly, she had the urge to slap him and did; the bewilderment he felt was almost great enough to make him soft. Still he finished, rolled off the condom, dropped it in the trashcan, drank a sip of water. All this as though she hadn't hunted the night only a few hours before for a predator to help himself to her body, her life.

♦

The man at the bar looked like Liam might have had life been less generous, less forgiving. His eyes were Liam's shade of blue, but with more shadows; a beautiful nose like Liam's, except one of his nostrils was slightly narrower than the other; his hair still a dark black whereas Liam's had begun to gray in his early twenties. He had all the right features to make a handsome face if not for his thick lower lip which extended too far out like that of a pouting child, his pupils darting rapidly as though the empty bar was a moving train. He looked at the perspiring drink in his hand and swallowed the air, his Adam's apple ascending and descending. Eve was at the other end of the bar. She crossed and uncrossed her legs in a way to let him know she was open to conversation.

He spoke rapidly, asked predictable questions. The combination of arrogance and desperation seemed the reason for his loneliness, his inability to attract women despite decent looks. She mumbled replies, put her elbow on the counter, cocked her head and nodded as his words became white noise. She drank. She knew that he wouldn't notice she wasn't listening and also that he could hold a monologue forever if she didn't stop him. She also knew that he was hopeful. The alcohol coursed through her blood, loosening her limbs. Her blinks were slow.

Eve thought to herself that it wasn't wrong—she wasn't being disloyal to Liam because she found this stranger repulsive. And she needed to allow for chance, if only once, to determine whether or not she should be a mother.

If the impossible happened with this chance-of-a-person, this man who slightly resembled Liam, Eve told herself she'd had an abortion once before so she could do it again. She believed her calculations logical and ignored the rage in her body, its savage hope.

♦

On the train platform, her body shivered with the anxious excitement of being looked at. It was strange to be seen again and reminded that she was young still. Liam's phone calls had stopped completely. She decided to come find him in the city. A surprise.

Eve believed her life began the moment Liam picked her up off the ground, the blood from her head staining his shirt, but perhaps she had died then. The product of their relationship was born of a cheap trick carefully executed like a magician collapsing a birdcage with a dove still inside and presenting an empty cage to the delighted audience. *Where did the bird go?* Such infinite speculations and infinite possibilities. While in the actual cage, the dove had been slammed between metal bars, organs and veins crushed, all possibilities extinguished.

She was content to be a substitute for Pari, or another if not her, as we all were imitations of someone else, someone who might have drifted across the path of the person we loved. She'd convinced herself of their cowardice, if not bad fortune, and her own noble intention. She'd hoped that her loyalty and persistence would weather against other outcomes Liam could have had, other families, other deaths and loves. All enduring relationships rested on one necessary lie. Over their years together, she'd grown arrogant, certain that she'd entrapped the butterfly and held the world static.

So much effort it'd taken that there was little energy left. Eve boarded the train, sat down by the window, and pulled the suitcase containing Dog's stiff corpse inside close to her.

A stranger sat down next to her. Eve pushed the suitcase against the window to make room.

"Thank you," the man said.

He looked in his mid-thirties. He wore a well-tailored suit and carried a briefcase, an old-fashioned gesture since not many companies required such attire anymore. They fell into an easy banter, as people who find each other attractive tend to.

"What are you coming into the city for?" he asked after a while.

"I used to live there."

"So did I. There seems to be an expiration date for everybody— it's not easy to stay."

"Or to leave," Eve said. "It was hard for me."

"Are you moving back then?" He eyed her suitcase.

"I'm—" she began. "I'm looking for someone who is gone."

"That doesn't sound very promising."

Eve laughed, a little manically. The stranger joined in. She felt simultaneously the urge to take him out to a field of discarded industrial parts and fuck him until they both went blind with rage and the more pressing desire to push him onto the train tracks, burying his screams in the screeching of machinery pulling to a halt. She couldn't bear the threat of change.

"Do you think, perhaps, I could see you again?" the stranger asked. "Unlike whoever it is you're looking for, I'm easily accessible, however you want to reach me, by text, by phone, online—whatever app—I've got them all." He waved his phone, smiling.

How easily people did this, stars crashing into other stars, changing the course of human history without the blink of an eye. Once, she would have followed anyone home, thrown herself into the unknown, and each encounter had changed her.

"No," she said.

He smiled, not taking offense. She was almost charmed enough to change her mind. Then in an act of primal aggression, he pulled a marker from his briefcase and wrote an address on her jeans.

"I'll be there every night from seven to nine," he said.

◆

What time did to memories: reconstructed suffering and wove painful experiences with intermittent joy. Eve longed for specific tortures, their arousal of the nerves, her submission to the senses.

After giving birth to Blue, she'd craved dirt with the intensity and hunger of an addict, as though it had always been a part of her nourishment and now suddenly withdrawn. She pictured digging her fingers into the dark moist, feeling the earth push up underneath her nails, smearing a fistful on her face. She shivered with the imagined grains and rock shards crushing against her molars, the sound of them warm in her jaws, her ears. In reality, Eve held back. She resisted the same way an alcoholic turned from a drink in a chronic state of quitting. She was becoming thinner and thinner, weighing less than she had before the pregnancy.

One night, when Blue was a few months old, while Liam was sleeping, she went out to the garden and dipped her fingers in a mound of dirt. She'd thought that feeling its wet with her hands would be enough, but her stomach burned even more than before. Liam found her slumped over, her neck sticky with saliva. He crouched down beside her, pleaded, "Please tell me what you need, Eve. I'll do anything." He encircled her wrist with his thumb and forefinger. "But we can't go on like this—we can't—"

"I'm hungry," she breathed.

"So eat something. Let's go inside. I'll make you anything. Ramen and spam?" It was a favorite of hers once while she was in college. He used to tease Eve about her preference for gas-station food. Liam looked up at the black sky as though he already knew her wishes.

He tried to pry her fingers open, but she growled a deep-throated animal sound that made him pull back his hand.

"Is this what you want?" Liam dug up a palmful of earth and grass, held it to her mouth. Eve relaxed her lips, which she hadn't realized were so tightly pressed together that they bled when opened.

"Eat," he demanded. In his voice, she heard both pity and rage. He pushed one dirty finger in her mouth, spread the soil around the inside of her cheeks. Liam's face watery and exhausted.

She'd drained him of love, perhaps of compassion too. What was left—survival. He used his finger as a spoon and fed her like she was a child, his child, and cupped his hand over her mouth, shoving in more than she could swallow. She fell back, her head on the ground, her face to the sky. Liam leaned his weight into his hand, didn't let up as she coughed and coughed.

Tears filled her eyes, or his? Liam's features were blurred like the first time she saw him up close. It felt as though it had been years since they really looked at each other. She stopped struggling.

The roof of her mouth, her tongue, felt like shreds, like blood. He let go, trembling, apologizing.

"I'm sorry, Eve," he cried. "I don't know what overcame me. I don't know, I don't know—"

"You remember," Eve said. "Ramen and spam. I didn't know you'd remember."

He picked her up and carried her inside. They slept well that night; they slept without waking.

In the morning, Liam knelt beside Eve, stroked her spine as she vomited on the rug, not making it to the bathroom. She sat in her own blood, which had not stopped since her giving birth, leaking from her underwear down her ankles, soaking her nightgown, the carpet. Getting a child didn't look so different from getting rid of one.

Diamonds of light blinking on the walls,

Blue's screams,

Eve's closed eyes,

Liam's breath at the base of her neck,

They were encapsulated there, within each other's helplessness, within the light, the piercing scream, a willful darkness, oxygen.

They told themselves that it was simply their youth, their inexperience, their self-imposed isolation. They blamed everything but the idea of Eve and Liam as a unit. They refused to even approach the thought that *they* were a mistake. She folded into the dark corners of their house, into herself. The thick silence punctured by sudden screams, Blue's, hers, his. She never saw the father and son, spending most of her hours in the bedroom. She'd relinquished all responsibility for her child.

When Liam came to the door, said, "Do you want to see him? Just for a minute?" she screamed back *Doyouwanttoseehimjustforaminute.* She echoed all his words until she heard the fading of footsteps.

Away, away—

At night, she crept out to the garden, gorged herself on dirt, felt renewed, until the next bout of nausea. Liam hadn't asked how Blue was possible when he had been so careful. She murmured words to no one, prayed that he was Liam's son, prayed for what she was unwilling to accept.

Eve didn't know how much time had passed when Liam returned. She smiled to let him know she had no strength left to scream. He set down a bucket of water and a hand towel by the bed. Without speaking, he removed her gown, underwear, socks. She watched him closely for signs of horror at the state of her new body, which she herself was too afraid to look at, but his expression was serene, as still as the coldest mountainous lakes. He wet the towel and wrung out the excess water. He wiped her body inch by inch, toe by toe. Gently, he scrubbed away the two lines of dried blood caked to the sides of her thighs.

"You don't have to hide from me," Liam said.

He lay down beside her, let out a sigh, and closed his eyes. She reached for his fingers. Encouraged by his warmth, she ran her hand over his chest, his stomach, his groin. When she discovered his penis already hard, she laughed.

"Don't ask," he said.

Eve stroked his cock to show her gratitude. As his flesh swelled in her palm, she whispered words of pain and lust, wet words that salivated the senses, words to conjure worlds, words that stabbed and soothed. Liam came, his body trembling with the violence of earthquakes. She knelt between his legs and lapped at his warm release. She rested her head on his crotch and lay down with her body wedged between his legs. They fell asleep listening to the other's silent cry.

◆

From dirt he came.

◆

Liam's furniture store, its spotless glass front, its spare display, and its measured simplicity, exuded his temperament, his control. Eve had gone straight there from the train station. She asked the two salespeople, a woman and a man behind the transparent counter, where Liam was.

"We were actually going to ask you," the man said. "He hasn't been in for a long time, maybe a month, and he isn't returning any of our calls."

"We would have contacted you sooner," the woman added. "But he told us never to bother him or his family at home."

The last time they spoke was almost a month ago; Liam had said he would come home if she needed. Eve dialed his number and got voicemail. She went to his office at the back of the store to check his work computer: hundreds of unopened e-mails. Had Liam disappeared? She couldn't help but chuckle to herself because if he had, she didn't know if he would want to be found. It felt a fundamental question, one that demanded a fundamental answer, but she was afraid that there were reasons, good reasons, for Liam—for anyone—to stop wanting the life they had and exchange it for another. She checked their shared bank account: no sudden withdrawal or deposit. But this told her little since he could have cashed a check from a client instead of depositing it.

His employees hovered at the door, offered to contact the police. The feeling was familiar, even comforting, as though she'd been waiting for it, for the stage to sink, the whole theater of their life drowned under its own construction.

"Mrs.—" The male receptionist said. "I'm sorry about Blue." The other employee looked down at her hands, then at Eve, sympathy ebbing on her face.

"There's nothing wrong with Blue," Eve said.

They looked at each other, a flash of uncertainty, "But we heard—" One nudged the other's elbow.

She went out the door before he could finish.

Eve left the suitcase with Dog in it on the curb. She'd wanted to punish Liam with their dead pet, but she'd waited too long. Blue sky, a piece of blue chewing gum stuck to the bottom of her shoe, blue lipstick—as reasonable a color as any, yet how scarce, Blue, Blue, Liam's son in every way but his genesis. *I'll explain later, I'll explain when you can understand*, she had promised herself.

When was it the right time to acknowledge an old lie? The deceit stacked beneath other half-truths, the necessary ones, and the unnecessary.

Her face was contorting in public, the corners of her lips miming monstrosity. She felt the muscles in her cheeks, her jaw gaping into a soundless scream. She started to walk toward Liam's old apartment, the same one he had carried her back to years ago; he hadn't wanted to give it up even after they moved out of the city. She started to jog, then sprint toward the image of Liam sitting at the kitchen table, his hand lit by a circle of light, his adept fingers above the circuit board, things unchanged, static. In this alternate reality, she had never asked him to enroll at her college. He hadn't pressed his own warmth between her legs.

Desire had afforded them no foresight—humanity raced

toward the chance of being loved and always would, despite countless examples of its ancestors' failures, not caring that it would be nobler, kinder to not see it through, to leave the potential untouched, unloved, unharmed.

If I ran fast enough, the earth's rotation would be behind me, in the past; I could outrun time, circle back to the start. I could find you. Whole as you were.

She looked everywhere in the apartment for a sign of Liam's anger, blame. She ransacked the cabinet, upturned cups for a note she imagined he would write, *Eve, is Blue mine?*

Eve, who,

What did I do to earn such a magnificent deceit?

Eve, how

She wept as she searched for him under the bed, behind the shelves, in the ceiling vent. The punishment was greater—an absence so thorough it left little to speculation. When she was done, his apartment looked upside down. She was ashamed of the disorder she caused to his personal space and immediately started to clean, straighten, put things back. She did everything furiously, quickly, so that in very little time the apartment was back to its organized desolation. Then she thought perhaps she hadn't looked closely enough, she'd missed an important clue and began undoing everything once more, spilling trash on to the floor and carefully smoothing out crumbled loose papers, receipts, for the sign of another woman, another life Liam had chosen.

I'm sorry about Blue, the employee's words echoed at the back of her mind. Why? Why?

She found a square of to-do list; the insignificant yellow lined paper made her heart leap. List-making was a habit of his—she felt his presence in the room then, in her hand. There were the usual grocery items, a reminder to fix the light bulb, send a blueprint to Ralph, and the last item: *Tell Eve.*

♦

The man from the bar half-dragged, half-carried Eve up the motel stairs. She hung onto him like a puppet, willing him to direct her movement. Why did the onset of laughter feel the same as that of tears? She hated him for his complicit hunger of the flesh, for how easily she knew it would be for her to get him to forfeit a condom with a gentle assurance. Risk underlies humanity's most basic instincts both to self-sabotage and self-multiply. They had gotten this far—the keys deep inside the lock mechanism. He was less repulsive now that he'd stopped speaking, knowing they were past conversation.

An easy fall onto the tightly made motel bed, the tucked-in corners. They didn't bother lifting the blanket. He fucked like a father would a girl who reminded him of his daughter, hesitant, ashamed, at times polite, at times with a demonic urgency, perverse violence. His rhythm, Eve's automatic moans, sent her under water, a deep calm. A gelatinous blue, like ink, rolled into her.

She closed her eyes, screamed when the deep blue was pulled out of her in ripples, in waves, with metal clamps. White lights.

Eve opened her eyes and a stranger's stared back.

"Are you all right?" he asked. "Did I hurt you?"

"Are you finished?" she said. He nodded. Eve smiled and pulled him down for a hug. She imagined telling him the truth, that she wasn't on any birth control. She thought about how little she would feel if she were to learn tomorrow that the man with his still limp flesh inside her had tried to hang himself from a light fixture and instead died of electric shock. The realization choked her. The depthlessness of cruelty was learned only by those who had surrendered to a love, an obsession. So few things in the world genuinely weakened us that submission wasn't so much a question as an involuntary bend of the knee, as one would before Eden.

The stain on the motel bed sheets was shaped like a pair of wings.

The man and Eve relished the silence after sex, its momentary clarity. Everyone knows the miraculousness of sex no matter how base or empty, the body vanished into myth, magnified to constellations.

She watched him carefully put himself back together: shirt, then underwear, pants, belt, socks, as though his clothes were that of an emperor and not ragged, soiled from his own sweat. He said that he wouldn't ask for her phone number because a woman who insisted on a motel even though he had offered his apartment had no intention of getting beyond the impersonal. When she didn't contradict him, he went on.

"I know it's nothing special," he said, ripping open a packet of peanuts the hotel provided and poured it down his throat. "If it weren't me, it would have been another man."

"You're wrong about that. It had to be you," she said. His back straightened and his shoulders rose slightly. "If I hadn't seen you tonight, I would never have done it."

"Why?"

"You look like him, so much like him in many ways. It's the only way it would work."

He was silent. Probably he thought she was mourning a breakup, a death.

"I'm sorry," he said. "For whatever happened to him, to you. But I'm glad to know I reminded you of him and that you loved him. If my doppelganger found you, then maybe I'll find your doppelganger too, right?"

She acknowledged his statement, the kindness behind it. She thanked him. She took the subway afterward, walked the shortest route home instead of her usual meandering through the park.

She was lucky Liam wasn't home. She couldn't look at him then and thought only of another. *Blue, I'll name him Blue,* she decided.

♦

To dirt he returned.

♦

To cheer Eve up after her abortion, Pari told her stories of orphans in India, of girls she knew from high school who kept their unwanted pregnancies to end up in dismal situations.

"Like what?" Eve asked.

"Exactly," Pari said. "You never hear about them again. Getting knocked up is their last big news."

"I'm not sad," Eve declared, her face to the wall. And she didn't think she was. Aside from a heavy bleeding afterward—though nothing that couldn't be absorbed by a sanitary pad—she'd felt only the ghost of pain.

"I know," Pari said, tucking herself in next to Eve under her comforter because she knew Eve would again refuse to go out. It had been three days since her abortion, and she wondered if she would always be incapable of wanting something badly enough to become one of those girls Pari scorned.

When they stopped scrounging the after-light back alleys, stopped bargaining their girlish youth for a taste of the acrid, the sweet and obscene, Pari began to study in earnest. She approached the work with the same severity and focus as when they were dancing, swallowing pills, blinking away the time. For a while, it seemed they would never return to that dark punctured by neon lights.

Eve sat on her bed and sketched Pari's profile as she hunched over an enormous biochemistry textbook reading lines and pausing dramatically as though they were from a play. Eve pretended to listen while drawing her friend's eyes, lips, chin, again and again, overlapping one on top of another. Pari's studiousness was paying off. The professors, mostly men, wanted to save this beautiful, talented girl from her own self-destruction, so they excessively favored and praised her for work that was normally expected from other students. Eve's own grades were slipping, but she didn't know how to return to class, sit on hard chairs and listen to lectures with the same mild curiosity and indifference she once had. Everything took on an unbearable significance because she'd chosen it, this childless path.

She stayed in her room more and more. Her earlier sketches of skies, birds, streetlamps, objects she found during the course of a day were reduced to Pari in a towel after showering, the steam still rising from her damp skin, Pari sucking pasta sauce off her fingers, Pari slipping a bra strap off her shoulder, Pari. They were in their last semester of the first year. Pari didn't know yet about the drawings; Eve was trying to be as discreet as possible as she spied on her roommate. She wondered if she'd begun to admire her before or after she tried to render her image, before or after she realized that she couldn't bear a day without her friend in her frame of vision. Eve still didn't think herself an artist, but the idea had taken on an appealing shape—she imagined a lifestyle that afforded her to sculpt, paint, and continually search for the perfect medium for her singular subject.

Spring swifted by, dissolving icy branches as well as their habits, then summer—Pari announced she was going to her parents' home after exams ended. Eve tried to persuade her to stay, but she'd grown tired of waiting for Eve to get well.

"Please," she resorted to begging. "I'll go out with you every night like we used to." Pari was moving between the closet and her suitcase on the bed.

"I need a break."

"A break from what?"

Pari looked at Eve, cocooned in her comforter, her back against the wall. "When was the last time you left the room?"

"Thursday."

"That's a lie." She pulled out a pile of dirty clothes Eve had stuffed under her bed as evidence. Then she went back to the closet, removed her green sweater, her favorite.

"You're bringing that? It's hot out. How long are you planning to go for?" Eve couldn't hide the desperation in her voice.

Pari shrugged. She kicked the blanket away from her, yanked her legs free in an attempt to get up, to show her Eve's lethargy was finished. She'd accidentally kicked her manila folder onto the floor. Three months of sketches spilled out. She got onto her knees, gathering them onto her lap as quickly as she could, but Pari had seen them.

"I'm sorry." Eve trembled.

Pari took them from her and thumbed through each page, her eyes round and bright, her expression softening.

"Sometimes I draw," Eve explained. Then when Pari didn't respond, Eve repeated herself, "I draw sometimes." She was embarrassed by the pictures, of their vulgar lines and shading, their flatness. She knew she was far from producing a Pari she could be proud of.

Pari picked up the last page and handed it to Eve. "Do you want to come with me? I would love it if you came."

Eve let out a sigh of relief.

Eve's skin was joyously sunburned that summer. She and Pari were content being in the backyard of her parents' home, squinting up at the drifting clouds, raising their legs and watching sun rays spill through the gaps between their painted toes. Sometimes they rode the metal horses on Pari's rusting carousel—a childhood relic and absurd present from her father when she was five, its inner wheels groaning as they revolved in never-ending circles.

Eve now openly drew and sketched Pari in front of her. She could tell that her friend relished the attention, at her repetitive looking and unlooking, memorizing and returning to the page. She also started to include others whose gazes lingered on her friend: Pari's stepfather standing at the second-floor bedroom window, the pianist, the butcher, a little girl at the bus stop. This double vision magnified her, and Pari began to behave like a portrait in a painting. A stillness descended on her. She would suddenly stop moving and stand for several minutes without appearing to swallow or blink, as though waiting to be captured, memorialized. At night they studied Eve's day's work together.

"This guy wasn't staring at my breasts, was he?" Pari said as she eagerly looked at one drawing. "I thought we were having a nice conversation."

"He looked," Eve said.

"How about him?" She pointed at another figure.

"He looked too."

Pari rolled onto her back. She sighed, pretended to be offended. They carried on like that for hours.

Eve began to realize the power the images had over her friend, their ability to shape her reality. One day, she was sketching Pari as she was taking a deep dive in the lake, and Eve stopped, putting her pad and pencil aside. Pari got out and stood over Eve, the water on her skin dripping on Eve's face.

"What are you doing?" she asked.

"Napping."

"But the drawing—Will you be able to do it from memory? I can jump back in."

"That's not necessary," Eve said. "I'm going to stop drawing for a while."

Pari stood like a statue, as hushed as the lake behind her. After a little while, she said, "What does that mean?"

"I'm just sick of it. That's all."

"You know you can't just stop now. You've gotten so much better and in just a few weeks of practice."

The truth was that Eve didn't really want to stop, but she needed to know if Pari needed her to keep going. She wanted more than to depict their daily scenes. She wanted to merge them with her own inventions. But Eve shook her head, a little pleased at seeing Pari's frustration.

"I wanted it to be a surprise, but maybe I should just tell you now: I entered your drawings in a contest," Pari said. "If you win, your work will be exhibited for three days in Florence."

"What?" Their roles were now reversed. Just when Eve thought she had control.

"Eve, when we go back to school, you need to switch your major."

Eve should have known it wouldn't be enough for Pari to have pictures of herself drawn and sealed in a notebook, kept folded and tucked away. The future, the one Pari wanted, would bind them together forever, Eve as the artist, Pari as an object of beauty, one exalted. Eve found it hard to breathe and she realized then that drawing Pari hadn't made her happy; it was something she'd done in a chronic state of thirst, hopeful that the next picture would be the last. Privately she'd been longing for a future when she would no longer need to look at her.

"I'm not doing any of that," Eve said weakly. But she would win the contest, she would go to Florence, she would chronicle her friend's life for the next few years—she would because life demanded to be lived in perpetual resistance, in blissful misery. And who was Eve to resist the pull of friendship, its merry-go-round rotation as faithful as the earth's own?

◆

Tell Eve.

The sun had set. Eve sat on the floor of the apartment, looking at every object around her, not looking. What did Liam plan to say? A knock at the door. Eve listened intently to make sure she hadn't imagined it. Another knock, then her mother's voice, "Eve, I'm coming in."

Eve asked coldly, "What do you want?"

"They called me. The people at Liam's shop said I might find you here." Eve's mother's face was wrecked with worry. Eve turned away. She couldn't bear to look at her mother. She'd come in a hurry; she'd forgotten to draw her brows. She didn't look like her mother. The woman before her knelt down, put her jeweled hand on the side of Eve's face; she could see the sparkles of her rings in her peripheral vision.

"Do you want to come with me to a fashion show this evening? It might cheer you up," she said.

"A fashion show? I haven't seen my husband in more than a month."

"Well. Everyone has their own way of dealing with loss." When

Eve didn't respond, her mother added, "You're a woman now so I can tell you. After your father—"

"You slept with a bunch of different men," Eve said.

"What do you think I should have done, Eve? Wait for someone I'd only met once?"

Eve shook her head. "You wouldn't. You would never completely give yourself over to anything."

Her mother shifted, and her perfume penetrated Eve's nostrils.

"Come to the show," her mother repeated.

"How can he just disappear? He knows I need him. He knows Blue needs him."

"Eve, listen to me," her mother said, a new sternness to her voice. "Blue is gone. He has been gone for almost a year now and you need to acknowledge that. Your husband cannot deal with the death of his son alone while you carry on living in a different reality."

"He's not dead. Just because he stopped talking doesn't mean—"

Her mother's hand, her ornamented fingers, struck the side of Eve's face. She touched her cheek, surprised at the sting, glad she was still capable of pain. Blue, Liam's son and not his son—his chances had been slim since his conception.

"I'm sorry, dear. I am," her mother said. "But you can't deny death. It's not just a picture. I've always regretted your finding that photo of your father. . . . You've always gone on imagining what was never there. But you can't deny this."

Eve struggled to remember the last time she'd seen Blue, by the fireplace, with Dog, in the kitchen, in the burnt house under the gash of the roof. It had started raining, Eve told him to scoot over where the roof was still intact. She saw him everywhere and all at once. By the lake.

Eve shook her head. She couldn't remember the last thing he said before he'd gone silent—those last words, what were they?

She stared over her mother's shoulders to the kitchen, listened to the regular hum of the fridge. Her mother hugged her, a ridiculous gesture. Eve's left ear against her mother's chest, the unbearable loudness of her heart beating. Eve wanted to laugh, but instead cried, and the hilarity of her tears made her cry even harder. She thought, *My poor mother, she would need to change her tear-soaked blouse before the show.* They stayed like that, clasped together in that airless tunnel.

Eve was remembering, memories brilliantly white, blinding headlights. Liam's warning, *Something is bound to go wrong with our child,* but nothing did; he was a healthy boy whose heart stopped beating due to neglect. And the irony—the flash of release that betrayed Liam's expression when he realized Blue wasn't his, theirs, but Eve's and Eve's alone. Her responsibility to bear. And still, Liam had buried Blue alone, this son of hers, too much of hers.

Eve's mother took out a bag of chestnuts from her purse, peeled the shells and demanded that Eve eat. It was one of the few gestures that betrayed her age—her tendency to force-feed the young, criticizing them for their thinness while her own body was long and slim, her skin taut against bones. She wore her clothes in a way that displayed their shape instead of her body, emphasized their elegance rather than her own. As a child, Eve had marveled at how differently she appeared in each outfit and was terrified when she caught her mother naked. Beneath layers of textiles, a flatness that mirrored deserts.

Eve chewed the nuts, their sweetness coating her gums and teeth as her mother dotted her face with a pale makeup, smearing it thickly over her inflamed cheeks. She called out the name of each item as she applied it on Eve, *After Party, Ordinary Sunset, White Fire.* Eve disappeared inside her chatter, relaxed under her touch. Her mother was an expert at conjuring beauty; she had a gift for playing with light and shadow that could trick even the most perceptive eyes. She stood Eve in front of the mirror, admired the result of her work. Her hands were on Eve's shoulders, her gaze penetrating their reflections so deeply that Eve felt the mirror would crack.

"It's my fault—I thought you needed time alone after, but that was the last thing you needed," her mother said, gentler than Eve had ever heard her. "You know me. I was never any good at comforting you."

Then, as though she'd had enough of her own emotions, her expression changed.

"Something's not quite right," she said. She shook off her jacket and draped it over Eve's shoulder. "Look. Just look. This is you." She smiled, satisfied.

Eve knew the reflection was only an illusion, colors and shades bending, tilting her features into conventionally pleasing standards, but it didn't bother her. She served beauty, the beholder instead of beholden—it was a better place to be. Eve asked her mother why she hadn't covered up the swollen dark circles under her eyes.

She smiled. "A little appearance of suffering isn't always bad." Then she stepped away from Eve, circled the apartment, and sat down on Liam's bed.

"There's no sign of you here. Nothing to suggest an artist ever lived here," she concluded. "It's dismal."

"We spent a lot of time here, but it was his long before I came."

"He kept this apartment when you bought a house in the country. Why?"

"For work," she said, and her stomach tightened as though she'd told a lie. Liam had loved the country's wind and sun but always returned to this apartment where windows were painted shut, the air trapped inside, time held static. It seemed Eve had never been able to ask difficult questions of Liam, those with answers she didn't want to know.

Eve followed her mother down the stairs of the apartment building, their heels striking the steps—each harsh echo a point of reference for the future. Blue was dead; Eve was walking down the stairs. Liam had disappeared, but the sharp points of her mother's shoes, their concrete reverberations, were consistent and pressing, propelling her into the next second, the next moment, the absolute conviction that if she reached far enough into the future, *their future*, she would touch the past, time only a circular map.

Blue's shoulder blades as delicate as bird wings, Liam pushing against the weight of water, the weight of tears, into the lake and at the same time holding Eve back, screaming at her not to take a step further because she couldn't swim.

She didn't see Blue, not the foam on his cold lips, not the bulging blue eyes. Liam had wrapped himself around their son, folded his own flesh into Blue's, and kept screaming, piercing, senseless guttural sounds because the silence, the stillness was unbearable, *Don't look, Eve. Don't look*. Even then he was protecting Eve. But from what? *He's not breathing, he's not breathing, Eve. Eve.* The completeness of *Nothing*, the long-forgotten whys came back, bricks falling from the sky's vault, crashing into earth, *Why work? Why marriage? Why children? Why.*

Eve thought she understood then—how life must accrue and empty. How impossible it was to save beauty from decay. Then immediately, those thoughts were replaced by other thoughts more sublime: the idea that this hadn't happened, that she could reverse the scene before her, keep it from carrying out. She retreated, her foot on her own shadow. She left the field, left Liam and the corpse of their son—the story she'd not chosen.

She went back inside their house and sat at the kitchen table. She stared into the creases of her palm, *Tell me, Eve.* She had done this so many times before, going inside the alleys of her mind, camouflaged knowledge with invention, stepped back in time. Reversed death. Outside, the howl of an animal, its wet and heavy footsteps approaching. The damp weight Liam carried in his arms. He pushed the door with his shoulder.

"Help me," Liam whimpered. "Call someone. Please, Eve."

Eve looked away from the shapes of them. The wet drips of Blue. There was a finite number of original inventions a mind was capable of. A damp gray mist spread across her vision. She would abandon everything for this final story.

♦

She was good at it—reality something to be sculpted and carved: a child made out of clay, a muddy child whose fingers curled or elongated depending on the day, whose lips never opened. He was something all mothers wanted: a child that never grew old. She dipped her fingers into warm water and smeared her hand over the sculpture's face, her thumb erasing its eyes, her nails gouging out its cheeks. She was getting closer. She would bring Blue back.

Outside, in the shed, Liam too was hard at work, cutting slabs of wood, sanding and polishing. He had convinced the morgue to keep Blue for two days while he built a coffin for his son. Liam had not bothered to wear safety glasses, his neck close to the blade as he fed it raw pieces of wood, his face white from the sawdust the machine kicked up. He had cut down the tree, the one where he had put up swings for Blue, where he had excitedly planned for a tree house once Blue was older. Liam nearly finished the coffin, but something wasn't quite how he pictured it if he could have pictured anything like this—the grains didn't run in the right direction, the colors too bright. This was his third try and he needed to get it right; he was running out of time.

At night, under the dim light bulb, they ate stale bread together. Liam drank expired milk from the carton and said nothing about its sour taste. They were balancing on a tightrope. Words felt like knives, daggers slicing open the dark belly they were in. They were miserable in their silence, so they cleared their throats, opened and slammed shut cabinet doors, threw cups in the sink and listened as the ceramics cracked against metal.

"I'm going to shower," Liam said. Eve nodded. Minutes later, she found him in bed still in his work boots. She lay down, inched closer to him.

In the morning, he put the coffin in the back of the truck and drove off. He must have asked her to come with him; she must have refused. They must have argued until their throats were hoarse and Liam left, swinging the screen door so it broke for good this time. Eve went to her studio. She spoke to Blue as he materialized under her fingertips—and the pain, it must have been her pain, began to settle like flakes at the bottom of a snow globe.

She talked and talked.

As she coated him with paint and words, his eyes blinked open. She gasped and cheered. She knew it was possible. Perhaps she'd wished for this day to come, when she would realize the point of why she was who she was, of why she had the skills she had. When did Liam return? How long had he been standing there, framed by the opened door, only a few steps from Eve, an interminable distance? She turned to him; joy burned and streamed down her face. *Look, my love. Look*, she said.

Liam's face crumbled. Golden light on his lashes, on his lips, his cheekbones. Light saturated his face. Blue veins underneath his skin. *Veins*, Eve thought and turned back to her son, her sculpture.

No, Eve. No.

Blue's fleshy surface needed more than just colors, it needed light, it needed *veins*. She dipped the paintbrush in a dense white, silver, and a pigment that had perhaps loomed in the imagination for centuries but wasn't available to artists until much later—cerulean blue.

I can't lose you too, Eve.

Eve got up and pulled Liam next to her. They stood together facing the new Blue, their hands intertwined, the lattice of their life tightening. She felt Liam weaken; the muscles on his face yielding—he didn't know exactly what she was asking, but he was perhaps too exhausted to resist, too frightened of what it might do to deny her this. What of reality, but the one our lover weaved in their sleep, what of blindness, but a different way of seeing.

Look, my love. Look.

◆

Liam lay on his back on the lawn and used his shins to lift the child sculpture against a white sky. Airplane. Blue didn't move because he could not. He didn't speak because his heart, lungs, and blood were made of mud. This was what it took to survive.

◆

At dinner, Eve set the table for three. Liam put the sculpture in the empty chair between them. They talked about painting the house, turning over the garden's dirt, chopping up more wood to prepare for the winter. They talked as though they were newlyweds and the property an exciting project full of possibilities. They ignored the gray dampness that had permeated the walls, the floorboards, the broken light bulbs they wouldn't replace. Eve spooned more food onto Blue's plate in front of the sculpture.

"He isn't eating," she said.

Liam didn't respond.

"Feed him," she demanded. "I'm not the only one responsible for keeping him alive."

Liam's hand shook as he brought the spoon near the sculpture's clay lips. Suddenly, he dropped the spoon and the food splashed on the floor.

"It's okay—" she said.

"It's not okay, Eve. It's insane," he said. Although he didn't raise his voice, the anger in his tone made her scooch back in her seat.

"I can't. We can't do this."

"It's okay," she repeated. "It's okay. Please sit down."

"Look at that thing!" he said. "That isn't him!" Liam shoved the table away with a surprising strength, knocking everything to the ground.

"You don't think I know that?" she said between gritted teeth, bending down to clean up.

"I don't think you do, Eve." Liam's voice was hoarse. "You've lost your mind and so have I for going along, for letting you do this for as long as we have."

Eve gripped a piece of broken dish. "Maybe you can't see how I need it. You can't really understand, can you? You're not in as much pain because he isn't even yours. It's simple biology." She spat out the poison, the ink-black truth that had been so long lodged in her.

"What?"

It spilled from her like gibberish from the possessed. The story—that was all it was—a well-kept fable that now murdered them both. Word by word, she robbed him of the only thing he had left: the right to grieve for his son. Liam leaned on the kitchen counter. Then, giving up, he crumbled to the floor. He screamed into his hands without restraint, without any need left for disguise, tears and saliva foaming from his lips as would for an animal during a seizure, clutched by impending doom and torn from its automatic will to survive, his admission of loss raw and trembling as Eve watched, as evening light flooded the room with an unbearable gentleness.

♦

"Who are you?" he said.
"Who are you?" she echoed.

♦

I'm going to the city tomorrow, Liam had said when he really meant he couldn't go on pretending, playing and talking to a lesser Blue, the always-mute sculpture. He grimaced at the lump of mud she continued to caress, to coo at, his heart brimming with sorrow and rage. The phantasm of Eve's mind, her reality, was folding before his eyes, infinitely inward—a puzzle box without solutions.

♦

He would leave for the city in a few hours.

The deep blue sky, threads of milky clouds: a heavenly ocean that would sink him. Toward the lights of the city he would go, where such obstinate beauty didn't exist, didn't remind him of death. He knew that once he left, he wouldn't know how to return. Like a boy playing hide-and-seek, he was standing behind a tree far from the house, out of Eve's sight. The child sculpture nestled against his chest, its mute heart, silent breathing, forever open eyes—an atrocity—and yet, he had surrendered to Eve's will.

He had thought it was kinder to play along, allow her time to adjust to Blue's absence, but their pretense had only become more elaborate, Eve retreating further and further into the recesses of her mind. He held the hideous sculpture up to eye level, whispered goodbye; and in one motion, with all his strength, smashed it against the tree trunk. He fell to his knees then, gathered the broken pieces together, and because he knew no one could see him, allowed himself to weep as he had when he was a boy, large sobs that sounded like laughter.

It was the end of imagination, the end of pretending that he had never grabbed those cursed drawings, masturbated onto the face of Eve's creation out of anger, humiliation, a wish to punish her for turning away from him and Blue, year after year, always sketching that same old face that sickened him. He had begged her to seek help; she'd hissed at him, saying, *How, exactly, do you imagine them helping me?* Please, just stop drawing, he'd said, realizing he sounded like a frightened animal, threatened by his wife's talents. Then, as though an invisible hand were tugging on the strings attached to his fingers, he yanked the folder Eve was hugging to her breasts. He ripped out the pages, turned on the stove, and lit them on fire as Eve screamed, got to her knees, crawled around the kitchen, putting out the balls of flame he had tossed onto the floor.

Where was Blue then?

Neither of them thought about the boy, who had been watching them from behind a door, hushed as a bird that had lost its song. Quietly, trembling, he had snuck out, went as far as the lake, went in the water because he thought he could seek refuge there for a while where he wouldn't be able to hear the violence in his parents' screams.

Liam grabbed a fragment of the sculpture and pocketed it. The tragedy was that he loved Eve, had loved only her, and was moving toward a life without her, a life of self-obliteration because he couldn't bear to look into her eyes, couldn't risk seeing there his own undigested devotion reflected back at him, couldn't accept that his love had not been enough to save them.

CARD TWO

THE SOFT SHACKLE

L iam held two glasses of champagne, the rose one for his newly wedded wife. He was taking it to her but delayed his steps so he could watch her stand by the arched window. So much light poured through the glass dome above her that he had to squint to look at her: a woman in white—an old-fashioned, even outdated, symbol, and yet it hadn't failed to stupefy him. His mouth quickly filled with saliva as he stared at the woman he thought he had completely lost any sexual appetite for. Pari's dress, which Eve had designed and sewn herself, had discreetly placed white feathers at the waist and on the shoulders across the back that made his wife look like a young swan.

To his surprise, Eve had come to the wedding. He would barely have recognized her as the girl who woke him in the rain when they were in Florence all those years ago if not for those wide, unblinking eyes, that look of adolescent surprise. She was a girl no longer; neither was she a woman, but a spirit in daylight—at once visible and invisible. He watched the two of them, Eve in a maroon dress, the color of graveyards and dirt, and Pari putting her winged wrist on her friend's. The sight of them together, like colored glass shards, ached him. He walked through the roomful of pats on his shoulder, smiling faces, approving nods, to be near them—the one he married and the one he could have loved—this indecipherable pair that made him feel a perpetual fool.

He handed the rose champagne to Pari, who pretend-sipped it. She wasn't ready to tell everyone the news; she'd told him that night when she returned from Eve's studio. He feigned a surprised reaction, although he'd already spent hours replaying the words he heard on the other side of the door. He had told her he was elated, because he was, and he'd felt a rush of affection for her then, the soon-to-be mother of his child.

Eve didn't greet him, only slightly softened her gaze. He smiled at her, at Pari, grateful for the complicated joy inside him.

"I wanted to congratulate you in person, but I have to go soon," Eve said, looking at neither him nor Pari.

"Don't leave so soon," Pari said. "It's going to be a bore without you."

A rare half-smile on Eve's face. She shook her head. "Really, Pari, you know the show is in two weeks. I'm supposed to deliver thirteen and I haven't finished a single one."

"Still, please stay," Liam said, surprising himself. Pari's grip on his elbow tightened.

Eve blinked. She looked at him without attempting to disguise the suspicion on her face. She must have thought, *What else will you do to me this time?* It wasn't as though he could repeat the horror of that night in Florence all those years ago. Such things could only die once.

"Please stay," he repeated, before walking away toward the other guests.

He focused on the fact that he was going to be a father. This wedding, he felt, was more for the unborn child than anyone else. He couldn't wait to meet him, to tell him about the way his mother looked in her swan dress. He would believe he was born of love; that was important. And when he became a man, he would expect nothing less. He decided then that he would be with Pari until the grave. Liam's story had ended, but his child's had only just begun.

◆

For the first time since his thirtieth birthday, Liam was on his own again. The eight years with Emily weren't entirely wasted, but he had hoped for something beyond his control, something to disrupt the tides. He had seen it happen to people he knew, this game-changing force, erotic and fatal. It had led his father into bankruptcy and then divorce; it nudged his friend over the edge of a mountain cliff. He had heard of its power to consume, to corrupt the innocent, to conquer the strong; it seemed to be everywhere, this force, yet it remained remote to him.

Emily was a nice girl, and they had managed not to despise each other, not to ever feel more than what was necessary to remain together. Maybe breaking up with her was a mistake. But for now, he wouldn't think about it—one of his strengths was the ability to compartmentalize. His uninterrupted years working, accumulating wealth for his boss, had afforded him a month-long vacation without any reproach. He could tell even his coworkers were glad to see him desire something other than to show up at his desk, always an hour early, every day for the last ten years. He was on his way to Europe: Germany first, then France, then Italy.

He marveled at his ability to crave something so abstract. Maybe it was a place and not a thing, somewhere that he had skirted the periphery of but never entered; it wasn't like him to want what he didn't understand. He believed he was born with some artistic capability, but he had always respected the logical and scientific faculties more. His job as a computer engineer allowed him to use both; he thought he had found the perfect compromise. That was another thing about him—he knew how to negotiate. Emily had once said that he was reasonable to a fault. So it was a surprise even to him when he told her that he would not be marrying her. When she'd asked "Why?" he'd responded, "I don't know." After that she threw the sushi she was eating at him, picked up more with her hands—salmon, yellowtail, a fried shrimp head, all flying in his direction. Even in such a moment, he couldn't help the thought that Japanese food was too costly to use as a weapon. For her sake, he wished it had been something more practical, like drumsticks. She insisted he tell her the other woman's name.

"There's no other woman," he'd said.

"Don't lie to me. I deserve the truth after eight years." She wept and screamed.

When she fell silent, he offered her a tissue. Her reaction surprised him; never had he thought himself capable of inspiring such hurt. He wondered if he could take it all back. *Why not spend your life this way?* He could make this compromise just as he had many others. Perhaps every few years he would have an affair—he could be quite content.

"There's no one else," he said.

"You're leaving me for nothing? For the complete unknown? I know you better than that." She grimaced, her face tear-streaked. "Don't expect me to believe that."

He kept repeating himself, thanking Emily for the time they had shared, but the more grateful he was, the more furious she became. She scratched the side of his face, drew blood, punched and kicked him, and when he tried to still her, she bit his wrist. He had never seen this kind of passion from Emily, and for an instant he was again consumed with regret.

"Please tell me. I can handle it," she begged. "I can understand if you're in love with someone else."

So he obliged her. He'd reached for the first word that came to mind, a biblical one, the name of the primordial woman. *Eve*, he said and felt an electric current ripple down his spine.

"Her name is Eve."

His lie took shape, inflated in the room, in the air between him and his now ex-girlfriend. Emily's pupils seemed to dance, hazel bleeding into green, amber glowing at their black centers. He realized what he had done—in seconds he had destroyed what took years and years to build. He understood then how unfair he had been and how he'd never given his relationship with Emily a real chance. There had always been the other woman, *Eve*, the imagined one whom he pegged Emily against.

Such a sudden loss aged him, made him more aware than ever that he was no longer as young as he thought. Forty-two wasn't the same as thirty or even thirty-eight. He had consumed enough self-help books, gone through enough steps on how to get over a break-up; now he was asserting a final effort, the one advice all the relationship gurus had in common: going someplace new and putting a physical distance between him and her.

On the plane, already skeptical of the journey, he decided that he would kill himself upon returning. It would be the last thing anyone expected of him, and it made him question the image he had been projecting his whole life. How envious he was of a suicide that might elicit understanding instead of bewilderment: *It makes sense. I might have done the same if I were him.* He felt enormous relief once he made the decision, closed his eyes and imagined the multiple ways calm would flood over him, eclipse his inability to see beauty.

In Germany and France, he eagerly visited the monuments, ate the food, drank beer and wine. He was proud that he could enjoy the varying decadence automatically, indifferently, the way he had always enjoyed sex with Emily without changing his mind about death. Each night, he found himself embracing a different woman, some whose company he paid for, and some he didn't, some treating him with a naked detachment that mirrored his own, others with such an optimistic sincerity that both comforted and filled him with shame.

He arrived in Florence exhausted, glad to near the end. Maybe he didn't need to return at all, maybe this would be the last ring at the center of the labyrinth—his resting place. He checked in at the hotel while considering his options. He tossed a coil of rope on the hotel bed and briefly inspected the light fixture on the ceiling. Tomorrow perhaps.

Outside.

Rain filled the cracks between the cobblestones. He wished for his body to liquefy along with these celestial droplets and drain into the gutter, but his death would be ugly and painful. He stood under the open sky for a while as though disappearing were a real possibility, as though on his last night he would suddenly discover in himself a superhuman ability, something heroic. A group of young people passed and a few turned to assess him—what did he look like to them?

He realized then he was no longer in command, his limbs, his hair, his thoughts had slumped into the past while he remained standing, mountainous and absurd, waiting for the clock to catch up with him. Someone—he couldn't see their face or, if he could, his mind in that state didn't bother to spatially arrange their features in a way that made sense: the nose seemed to float to the left of one ear, the mouth below the chin—this figure put an umbrella above his head. He didn't know how long he stood there, but he could feel his skin begin to dry while rain formed a white curtain around the edge of the umbrella.

"Do you speak English?" the figure asked. He nodded. The red mouth was moving into place, the eye returning to the side of the nose. "Do you need to call someone?"

He shook his head.

"I would love to stand here and keep you dry forever, but I have an art exhibition a block from here. It's in a shitty little basement and no one will be there, but I figure I should at least show up."

"Your art?" he said. The girl nodded. "What, mmm, is it about?" He was embarrassed that he didn't know the right question to ask an artist.

"Do you want to come?" the girl asked, putting her hand around his elbow.

He followed her along a narrow street, down a small flight of stairs, into a cave-like structure where he looked up and saw something that tugged on his departing soul and put it back inside his body, something both invisible and magnificent, something like beauty.

He was intrigued by the simplicity of the sketches, the artist's resistance to adding details, leaving plenty of negative space. All the images featured the same young woman and her spectator. Though the woman was undoubtedly attractive, he sensed something else was driving the images—the drilling focus of the gazes from her onlookers. He was unable to look away, making himself a participant as he stared at both the spectator and the young woman, feeling as though he had caught each in an intensely private moment. He checked the label for the price, though he already knew he would never own one of these—they all seemed to be accusing him. When he saw on the label the name of the girl who had unhooked her arm from his elbow and was conversing with the only other patron there, he walked over and interrupted them.

"Your name is Eve?" Liam said.

The other patron walked away and started to take pictures of the pieces.

Eve nodded. It was then that he began to take notice of her—this pale, waif-like girl who drew these unsettling works. She wasn't beautiful—her moon-shaped face made her look adolescent, her eyes a flat brown, her body seeming to float underneath her clothes. Still, she had a manner of looking at things with such intention, almost predatory, that made her appear larger even though she was smaller and shorter than him. He quivered when she looked at him. Thankfully, the other patron shouted across the room and Liam had an excuse to break eye contact.

"Who's the beauty in all these?" the man asked.

"My roommate—" Eve said, then added, "my only friend."

He hadn't realized the girl in the pictures was real. He knew then that his plan would be halted; he must see her, if only to give himself some peace of mind, to undo the feelings the images had stirred in him.

◆

Pari locked her arm around his elbow, squeezing him to her side as they navigated the crowded city sidewalk as a couple, dodging the human bullets that raced toward them. Neither of them spoke of that night in Florence. Returning home had sobered him. He wondered if the broken glasses, the drawings, the blue liquid-brilliance of the moon spilling on terrace had really happened. He told himself that the whole trip—his plummeting despair leading him to the decision to kill himself, the feverish freedom he felt, finding himself shielded from the rain by a girl whose face he couldn't see—could be summed up as a simple lapse of judgment, a well-known and well-acknowledged kind of crisis people go through.

He needed a little adventure, so he actively pursued what he had always ignored—his instincts—and let them overtake all other faculties he valued. He came back with a pretty girl, who wanted to hear him make promises, who kept him warm and distracted from all the questions that had tormented him for months. He stayed with Pari because the story sounded right when he told it, *How lovely that you two met in Florence and how serendipitous you both live in the same city.* His coworkers' admiration satiated him even though it was tinged with sarcasm—it was clear all the men were charmed by his girlfriend's plump lips, her straight white teeth, her easy, clean laugh. Perhaps a few of them even thought he didn't deserve such luck.

At night, when he came home from working late, a long-legged creature was already on his couch, offering opinions on matters he didn't ask to hear, asking how his day was and switching on the TV when he attempted to answer. He was pleased by his proximity to such corporeal beauty, its conspicuousness something he understood instead of feared. He tried to do better this time than he had with Emily. That meant he acted with passion, delivered a convincing portrait of a man in love, compensated appearance for what he failed to feel. His dreams of death returned, more vicious than ever, but he managed to silence them with sheer will and perhaps one more drink.

He avoided Eve.

Once at a restaurant with Pari hooked to his arm, they ran into Emily. She glanced at him, but mostly her eyes scanned Pari, her tiny waist accentuated by her tightly fitted skirt, her miles of legs even more exaggerated by high heels. Emily smirked, her face bright with contempt.

She came up to him, extended her hand to Pari, and said, "Nice to finally meet you, Eve."

He wanted to explain to Emily, to tell her *It isn't what it looks like, this isn't her*, but perhaps it would only cause her more pain to realize he had made up an affair to end their relationship. He was too flustered to realize he cared more about what Emily thought than Pari.

Pari frowned. Too confused to ask what this strange woman could have meant, she responded in a small voice, "Nice to meet you too."

At their table, once the waiter set down plates of food—grilled swordfish for Pari and pork chops for him—Pari hovered her silverware over the fish for what seemed like an interminably long time.

"You're not hungry?" he asked.

"Why did she call me Eve?" Pari said.

"Did she?" He straightened the napkin in his lap.

"You heard her."

"I don't know," he said. "When our relationship ended, she thought I was leaving her for another woman even though I wasn't. I don't know why she called you that. It's just her way of mocking me." He could have told the truth but found it unbearable to speak the name, as though its verbal articulation would give him away.

Pari took a bite of fish. She would have to accept his inadequate explanation. How often people ignored signs, irregularities in exchange for calm. She nodded.

There was no epiphany to be had.

◆

Sometimes after sex, Pari would ask about how he spent those first few nights in Florence, how he met Eve. His dismissive answers never satisfied her. One Sunday, after a particularly satiating sexual release, she pushed him, following up one question with another. He tried to speak casually but instead meandered, ended up describing the rain, how it poured in fine, translucent, silk-like strands. How his feet were soaked, yet he didn't feel any discomfort.

"She stood right in front of me, looking into my face, but somehow I couldn't see hers." He left out a few details: the rain, the tears that fuzzed his vision. "We went to the gallery after that."

"How ridiculous. You followed a woman you had just met," Pari said, laughing. "And a faceless one apparently." She mocked him, but he saw her expression had darkened.

"Maybe it was ridiculous, but I wouldn't have met you if I didn't," he said quickly to avoid a fight. That seemed to pacify Pari somewhat. She snuggled close against him, sighed as though exasperated by her own jealousy, suspicion.

The scent of her pineapple shampoo suddenly irritated him, as did her perfectly manicured toes. She had no physical flaw, her face terribly wonderful, her body rousing a lust deeper than he'd ever known, and all this maddened him. She had done nothing wrong except getting between him and his chance, perhaps his only chance, to love life with the clinging desperation of those who had just received their death sentence, to feel the way he imagined he had felt as a newborn.

◆

Pari saw Eve often, possibly more than she would let on. Liam knew that because upon returning from his trip he had sub-scribed to all major art magazines as well as a few indie ones and had them mailed to his office. Every few months, he would flip through them and find paintings of his girlfriend in different sce-narios, swallowing a bottle of pills, cutting her underwear into shreds, masturbating naked, her body sprawled across a landfill. Eve was, without a doubt, the artist. The expressions on the dif-ferent Paris disturbed him—none of them looked like the woman he lived with. It was as though Eve had inserted herself inside, invaded Pari's body with dabs of her own feelings, her paint. He tore out these pictures and kept them in his desk's drawer.

A part of him was waiting for Eve to send him a message, an email, something that acknowledged those innocent days of pure joy they had spent together. He told himself that if she contacted him just once, he would run to her, kneel at her feet, and beg her to forgive him. For one, two, three, then four years he waited, the drawer stuffed so full of ripped-out pages that he could no longer open it, but she stayed away, stubbornly, fiercely, so that he began to realize she would never exonerate him for what he had forced her to look at, his primal savagery something banal and grotesque, for what he had murdered at its moment of awakening.

♦

They probably spent too much time together for two strangers who had met in a foreign city. After a series of meetings for dinner, walks, gelatos, there were only so many choices remaining for a man and woman. They exclaimed repeatedly how they loved Florence, how they never wanted to leave. Every time one did so, they would look at each other, abashed at not being able to hide their mutual affection.

At breakfast, Eve ate little and responded to Liam's questions in monosyllables. She had spent the night in his hotel room, and he had fallen asleep watching an Italian movie neither of them could understand. They had kept a pillow-length distance between them. During the night, he'd startled awake, cock erect. He'd considered rolling to Eve's side and making love to her right then. After all, she'd been willing to share a bed with him; did she really expect nothing to happen? His lust overwhelmed him, jerking his limbs involuntarily, and yet at the same time paralyzing him to the mattress. Sweat soaked his back. He felt as though his heart was too, sweating. Thoughts tortured him until dawn pervaded the bedroom with its accusing light. He blinked, noticed that through all his deliberating and oscillating, his penis had gone limp long ago. He almost laughed.

The previous night's intimacy, its cautiousness, had somehow backfired. He sipped on his blood-orange juice and wondered if he should have at least kissed her, communicated something definite, but how could he kiss her in the way he needed to when he wasn't sure if he wanted to live? The coil of rope was neatly hidden in his suitcase underneath a stack of shirts. He put a croissant on her plate, which she peeled into shreds, giving him the distinct impression that he was tending to a child. Could she be the same person who drew those pictures? She rolled the croissant flakes between her fingers.

"Pari is coming today," she said.

"The girl from the pictures?" he said.

"You'll like her."

Over the next hours, Eve's mood steadily worsened. He suggested going out, but she didn't want to leave the room, so he quickly resigned to the idea of staying in all day—already he felt responsible for her well-being. She had dragged the comforter onto the floor in a corner of the room and made a nest there like a pregnant cat about to give birth under the stairs.

He had learned in the past few days, in pieces from their conversation, that Pari was the one who had orchestrated Eve's whole trip and that drawing her friend was the first and only serious artistic project Eve had attempted. He had expressed enthusiasm for meeting this pretty girl who, according to Eve's description, seemed like a self-inflicted mania, a compulsion that to him didn't sound much like friendship. Naturally, he was curious about Eve's friend.

A few nights before, he and Eve were on the floor, talking, looking at billows of wind fill and empty the white curtains. He had felt such peace that he almost confessed he wasn't supposed to be alive anymore, wasn't supposed to be speaking, whispering to this girl who listened to him as though his every faint inhale and exhale contained an enormous secret. He was surprised at how honest he could be when offered such priest-like attention. Eve had been silently nodding, but he sensed that she agreed with him, or at least wanted to.

He gave words to thoughts he never knew he had. And Eve—he loved saying her name—withholding the fact that he'd said it once before, conjured it like a spell—but what did it mean to adore a name?

Amidst that warmth, that idle serenity, he remembered something that turned him cold, something Emily had said during a fight. She'd called him *monstrous*, and simultaneously he'd felt his bones burst through his skin, saliva filled his mouth, ready to attack, sever the head of the woman who had been sleeping next to him for the last eight years. He realized then she couldn't have chosen an adjective more accurate—that was what he was—a beast that wanted only what it could murder. Next to Eve, his instinct faltered and waned—you could only kill something that wanted to live. He was baffled by the way minute details delighted Eve one minute and tormented her the next. They seemed to have this point in common: their lack of interest in surviving.

He imagined slicing her long, white neck open as she lay placid, unresisting, her stone-like eyes betraying no suffering—the fanatic's resilience. Was that love then—a lifelong rage suddenly subdued? And how long would this calm last? He battled between asking her to die with him or to marry him; such was the threshold he was on. Instead, he asked what her favorite color was, a banal question but one he thought might be important to an artist.

"Blue," she said.

"If I remember correctly, there wasn't any blue in your drawings. A lot of brown and red, but no blue."

"I'm saving it."

He told himself then that when he returned to the city, he would find her something blue that was also beautiful. Perhaps an exquisite silk ribbon she could use to tie around rolls of canvas.

◆

Before the wedding, he anonymously mailed his collection of magazine pages to Eve. A few of them had been marked with his cum over the years, sitting at his desk, stroking himself and marveling with disbelief that he and his fiancée hadn't fucked in months. It hadn't taken him long to tire of her beautiful shell.

Pari had become a fetishized object in the art world, people drawing new portraits of her based on Eve's work or reproducing the originals in a different format, but she responded to all inquiries that she would sit only for one person. The more exalted, eroticized she became in the public eye, the more vapid was her lovemaking. The walls of their bedroom were covered in different reflective materials, mirrors and gleaming fabrics. A kink Pari had developed. He knew well it wasn't so that she could see him from different angles; he had not aged well. He had developed a hunch from hours of working at a desk, causing a permanent back pain, his skin a chalkish blue, and though he still looked thin—an attribute he no longer took for granted—fat accumulated in strange places on his body. He had lost all motivation to keep up his appearance years ago.

While he thrusted slowly, aimlessly on top of Pari, she smiled at the ten, fifteen reflections baring their teeth back at her. She would orgasm no matter what he did, in spite of what he did. He had grown to care about her, to desire her attention even though he remained quite sure that his relationship and his world were small, *average*. That shock of hurt in his chest: when he proposed on his knees like some fool in the movies and Pari smiled that same smile she would at the ceiling, the walls, her doll eyes hollowing out his insides. He longed for the sweet, begrudging girl she used to be and that he hadn't wanted but who fell into his arms anyway. Was it his fault how things turned out?

One morning, Pari was getting ready to go do her usual rounds of meetings, interviews.

"Are you happy?" he asked her while brushing his teeth, as though it were as normal a question as any.

She glared at him and said, "Do you not want to get married anymore?"

"Of course I do."

"Then why would you ask me that?"

"Just wondering—"

"Of course I'm happy. Very happy," she said, walking out. It seemed it required some effort for her not to slam the bathroom door in his face.

From the window, he watched Pari exit the building before he leapt up and ran down four flights of stairs to catch up with her. He had never seen her alone like this, assured, walking alongside other rapid footsteps, her womanly confidence something new to him. He followed her onto the subway, up a crowded avenue that eventually narrowed into a residential street. He had never been here before, but he guessed from Pari's schedule that Eve's studio was in this concrete building. Its large, square courtyard was shielded from sunlight, emptied, without the sight of a single dead leaf, reminding him of a prison. He waited for Pari to close the gate behind her before walking up to check the names on the buzzer. He pressed all the buttons except for the one that said Eve, and eventually the metal gate propped open, letting him in. A rush of thrill and relief. Though he looked like any man climbing the stairs, he tried not to make a sound.

He stood in front of the door with the same number marked for Eve on the buzzer, feeling foolish and afraid of what he might discover and of what he might not. He pressed his ear flat against the wood panel and listened, hoping for a sign that showed his fiancée hadn't lost all interest in him. For a while, he heard nothing. Anxious sweat had soaked through the back of his shirt.

◆

In the studio, Pari put on her usual costume, smearing herself with handfuls of dirt. Her hair—which she had washed, detangled, and blow-dried into loose waves that morning—was now dripping with raw eggs and some pink pigment Eve had mixed in. Pari didn't know why she had bothered to shower, put on the silk blouse that had cost her a fortune and matching-colored shoes just to take them all off, and draped her body over the hard back of a chair still sticky from yesterday's slime, only that she needed it—the morning cleanliness. This project had taken Eve longer than any other—eight months of Pari leaving the studio with what looked to her like a finished painting only to come back the next day and to find that Eve had painted solid white over those hours of Pari's aching joints, twisted neck, her eyes burning from fatigue.

Still she came back.

She always came back. Perhaps Eve had realized that Pari couldn't stay away for long. A few years before, Pari couldn't finish her thesis to graduate, so swept up was she in the world of shattered light and vanishing shadows. It was true that she had pushed her body to the extreme for Eve, but what counted was what came afterward: the floodlight of admiration, adoration, and envy. Really it was the envy that she couldn't live without. On days when Eve was particularly severe, her demands puzzling to the point of being punitive, Pari dreamt of making it on her own, perhaps modeling a little or acting, but she knew the near-occult adulation she received was due to her proximity to Eve, their closeness, their refusal to work with anyone else. She would be stripped without Eve—the vacancy she had guarded beneath layers of the most exquisite textiles, her meticulously decorated face, would be exposed. She had to remind herself that her future husband, the one person who had detected this void, this silent vacuum syphoning on her soul from the moment they met, had chosen her over others. Over Eve. In his own way, she believed, he loved her.

"This looks about done," Pari gestured to the canvas, hopeful. "It looks—nice."

Eve put down her mug on a high stool, eyed Pari in a way that made her squirm. Pari shrunk into the chair.

"Nice?" Eve noised through the cracks of her lips. "Are you trying to spoil my day?" She dropped her cigarette in her mug. Pari imagined the sound it made as it sizzled off in the liquid, but she couldn't hear it. Her ears were hot as though Eve had put the cigarette out there.

That morning, Pari had told herself that she would finally stand up to Eve, she wouldn't let her friend belittle her again, but the courage she'd mustered when she was alone ebbed away in Eve's presence. No matter what Eve might say to Pari, she was convinced there was no one else in the world who needed her as much as Eve did.

Pari looked at the long streaks of gray lining Eve's hair, which she let fall down her back in tangles. Pari, who obsessively plucked any gray strands that sprouted on her head, didn't understand Eve's disregard, which made her look a decade older than she was. Still, her face retained that childlike expression often found on those trapped in that half-world between girlhood and adolescence.

"I didn't mean to upset you," Pari conceded.

Eve blinked, gliding closer, her ankle-length dress making her look as though she were levitating. She took Pari's chin in her hand.

"If you really didn't want to upset me, you would watch your waist. You're eating too much." She smiled. "I'm a painter, not a digital artist. Am I supposed to erase your bulging stomach? What exactly is that bulge that seems to get bigger every day?" Eve screamed this last question.

"You know what I eat." Pari began listing the meals she and Eve had designed together to keep Pari static, a breathing human sculpture.

"Do you hear that?" Eve asked. She looked toward the front door. "It's like the door is breathing—"

"Maybe I'm pregnant," Pari said. She hadn't taken a test, afraid it would force her to admit something she already knew.

"Maybe?" Eve was now gliding swiftly around the studio like an imprisoned spirit. As she moved, she knocked down paint tubes, easels, glass. She was no longer containing the volume of her speech, shouting from a deep hollow inside her. "Is it your boyfriend's?"

"Fiancé. And you know his name: Liam," Pari said, both fearful and strangely satisfied to reveal her engagement, what she'd kept hidden from Eve. "Who else's would it be?"

"With you, who really knows?" Eve said as though it were a genuine question without her earlier menace, all her energy suddenly gone. Her face pale, she reached for the mug with the moist, discarded cigarette and drank. Outside, the wind had picked up, lifting dead leaves and momentarily suspending them in space.

She looked out the window and saw a man walking rapidly away from the building, against the wind, all those dead leaves, his green overcoat recalling a taste, a forgotten delight, the sensation of warm rain permeating her pores, but not long enough for her to remember she had once been capable of more tenderness.

"I'm happy for you, really," Eve said, suddenly subdued. The smile on her face warm and helpless, a smile Pari hadn't seen in a very long time, not since those early days in college when they used to be as inseparable as shadow and light.

◆

Together Liam and Eve waited for Pari in front of the building where Eve had rented a room. He circled the piazza's fountain, tossed in coins, impatient for their wishes to be granted. Eve's anxiety had infected him; they wore their discomfort like armor. They were both so focused on feeling bad that he didn't see Pari until her knees were almost touching his. Her short dress, a mixture of robin egg's blue and viridescence, fluttered before his nose. He noticed the goose bumps on her otherwise velvety legs, probably from the chill. Immediately he was repulsed by the idea that she'd chosen to wear the dress despite the chilly weather, its impracticality, but still couldn't look away from her knees, her inner thighs. He could tell she was studying him too, perhaps wondering what his relationship to Eve was.

Eve seemed to deliberately ignore his and Pari's mutual curiosity and didn't introduce them, leaving him and Pari to exchange awkward pleasantries. The three of them entered the building's damp and echoey hallway together. The walls were graffitied, the stairs stank of bleach; why hadn't he noticed these things before?

In Eve's company, he had only paid attention to what pleased his senses, the perfectly preserved catacomb, the olive market, the perfume of magnolias in bloom.

For a moment, he considered fleeing, saying goodbye to Eve without asking for her contacts and leaving it up to chance to reunite them, but Pari had handed him her suitcase and purse so he had no choice but to follow them upstairs. He listened to Pari tell Eve about an art critic who had seen her drawings and telephoned Pari because she was listed as the contact. What luck it was that he happened to be an important reviewer for a newspaper, and now Eve might have a real chance at a career if she made the right choices. Pari added that she'd come ready to sit for Eve.

"I brought all my best dresses for this trip," Pari said.

Eve nodded. "You didn't have to. You look great in anything."

"Whatever. We can experiment—I could even pose with your new friend." Pari turned and winked at him.

"That's a good idea," Eve said.

To his surprise, Eve showed none of the anger around Pari as when she had talked about her. Instead, she disappeared completely, uttering only a few harsh whispers when she did speak, otherwise dissolving into the background as he and Pari took turns keeping each other entertained. At first, he felt unsettled knowing he was being watched and drawn, then surprised at how little time it took for him to forget Eve as she reduced herself to hands and eyes.

The three of them took a train to the ocean about an hour from Florence. It wasn't until sea foam grazed his toes, retreated, and again returned that he noticed Eve still had on her long dress. She stood by his side gazing at the shiny, tan bodies as though they were aliens, as though they possessed something utterly incomprehensible to her. She rubbed her eyes, looking confused. Pari was already in her bikini top the entire ride and had immediately taken off her jean shorts as soon as they heard the sound of waves breaking in the distance. She was swimming near a group of young Italian men. A large wave pushed them closer to the shore, where they stood half submerged. The men spoke; Pari tilted her head to the sky, laughing.

Liam turned to Eve. "Would you like to test out the water?"

She nodded, placed three fingers in his palm. Together they walked toward the retreating wave as though to chase it away. He rambled on about how much he loved the fierce sunlight even as it burned him, recounting memories of his boyhood summers spent by an endless expanse of blue. He described his friends, named them and their personalities, nights around a bonfire, green shards of broken beer bottles turned to sea glass. He talked until his experience no longer sounded singular but idyllic to the point of becoming stereotypical of a privileged upbringing—he couldn't help himself. When he finally realized Eve hadn't said anything in a while, he asked her for her first memory of the ocean.

"I don't know." She shook her head. "I don't swim."

"You mean you don't know how to swim?"

She nodded, offered nothing else except the blankness of her association with the sea measured against his exaggerated recollection. He blushed. Then he told her he needed to go for a dip and ran toward the foreign water. He was annoyed Eve had refused to meet his efforts to talk, to connect. Although he knew better, he told himself it was impossible for anyone not to know the ocean. He swam toward Pari, whose ease in the environment matched his. It was pleasant—she returned his enthusiasm, hung on to his arm as though she needed it. Every now and then, he glanced at Eve, who was flicking the sand with a stick.

It was almost dark when he and Pari came out dripping, wet with meaningless pleasures. Pari gasped at the massive labyrinth

Eve had traced on the sand and decorated with bits of shells and driftwood. Pari tiptoed within the lines for a while before giving up to go lie down on her towel. Liam's eyes locked with Eve's that seemed to challenge. He didn't want be humiliated, to never arrive at the maze's center, so instead he walked across the intricate paths, smearing them under his weight.

It would be many years too late that he realized Eve had not meant to mock him or undermine his way of loving the ocean. There were many ways to be at home by the sea and that was hers. Perhaps if he had understood her wordless attempt at relating to him, as close as she could to confessing that his feelings mattered to her, what happened next could have been prevented.

He blamed his carelessness on the dizzying heat, the too open sky. But there was something else, a fundamental truth, one he would never admit: he preferred a simpler kind of gratification, one he didn't have to decipher.

♦

Eve had stayed at the wedding after all. A few of the guests, mostly artists and journalists, encircled her. They introduced themselves as friends of Pari's and expressed a lifelong admiration for Eve's work. They asked about her projects, eager to demonstrate how intelligent and socially conscious they were through their questions. The younger, ambitious ones pulled on her fingers and touched her hair, overly familiar, as though her flesh contained the ingredient to fame, to success. A young blond boy, college-aged, had captured Eve's attention and would not release his grip any time soon. Liam watched the boy, saw something of himself there, and felt irritated at the fact.

The boy spoke as though he'd rehearsed his speech, of things unfamiliar to Liam: aesthetic theories, beauty and ugliness, his defense of Narcissus.

"I have photocopies of all your work," he exclaimed proudly as though he was the only one in that room who would. "It's interesting to see the evolution of your art, when it's laid out side by side."

"Is it?" Eve murmured.

The boy nodded, encouraged. "Your first exhibition in Florence: those drawings didn't show complex techniques, but they swept the art world by surprise, especially that one reviewer. I remember he said your art had 'an innocent wish to possess the beautiful and the immediate consequence of it.'"

"And what, exactly, is the consequence?" she asked.

"The power of beauty lies in its own vanishing—and you have immortalized it. You freeze it in time for others to appraise, stare at for however long they want."

Eve smirked. "What a clever way of complimenting and insulting me at the same time."

The boy blushed, his face lit with arrogance and anticipated victory. He continued, "Pari—your subject. Don't you agree she has changed over the years?"

"Everyone changes."

"Yes, but her metamorphosis, or I should say reverse metamorphosis, feels measured with each painting that you released, each showcase. I don't know if you ever read the articles about your relationship with her—there are many, but I mostly think they're horseshit."

"I've read a couple."

"You haven't read mine," he said. "I think Pari's life yields to the reality you shaped. The year you two were working on the landfill exhibit, people saw her on the street and mistook her for a homeless woman. Need I mention the three months she spent in the psych ward?" The boy glanced quickly at Pari, then returned his attention to Eve. "Her psychology—"

Around them, people were cheering, clinking glasses, exchanging flirtatious remarks. The roomful of beautiful faces suddenly seemed grotesque. Fraudulent. Everywhere were models, people in the entertainment industry and the arts, friends of Pari's. Even the ones with fewer blessed physical attributes made up for it in extraordinary outfits and makeup. Liam loosened his tie. He picked up a canapé and shoved it into his mouth, tasting nothing but salt. Suddenly, he felt like he didn't know what he was doing there. He stared at Eve, hoping for a returned look of acknowledgment of the strange situation they were in.

"She was just overworked; we both were. Anybody could break down. Besides, so much of what you're saying is just speculation." Eve finished the rest of her drink and stood up.

"That's a lot of power to have over a person. A *living* person," the boy insisted, taking hold of Eve's wrist. "It's a kind of psychic supremacy—your ideals, your dreamt-up nightmares have an objective force in Pari's mind. What you imagine becomes her reality."

Liam hurried to Eve then; it seemed moments before she would fall. He guided her away from the circle of eyes and ears that had heard the insolent boy's theory; where there was blunt admiration before, now their gazes were full of suspicion and, Liam detected, disgust.

"Academics," he said to Eve by way of comfort. "No different than madmen." He looked across the room to where Pari was posing as hundreds of cameras flashed at her. Some famous brand he couldn't remember had offered to custom-tailor her dress if she let them photograph her at the wedding and include the pictures in their upcoming catalogue. She looked content. Liam was used

to their birthdays and holiday parties becoming another opportunity for Pari's career and had come to expect it. Yet, he was
surprised at how exasperated it made him that they couldn't even
have this one day to themselves. It seemed her beauty was a kind
of mortgage that kept them in perpetual debt.

Liam walked Eve through the side door to the bride's dressing
room. He realized now that by coming to Eve with perfect timing,
he had admitted to watching her all night. He uncorked the wine
bottle on the vanity table, poured two glasses.

"I'm sorry about that. We should have been more discerning
about our guest list," he said. "But Pari has a lot of friends—
admirers—as you well know."

"I can't stand her," Eve said, gulping down the wine.

"What?" He was startled by her frankness, her childlike and
unfiltered hatred.

"Your wife." She sighed. "I don't know; it seems like she has
everything."

"It looks that way—" He faltered, once again not knowing how
to be in Eve's presence.

"She's pure fiction. I hope you realize that," she said. "That
kid wasn't far off. I haven't read his work, but I've heard of it. He
believes that I unconsciously manipulate my subject to my whim,
bend her reality because I don't have the courage to live my own,
because I love her too much and want to be under her skin, live
through her. The only thing he's wrong about is that I love her.
Quite the opposite."

"How can you—how can you say such things," he said weakly.
"She is your best friend. She would do anything for you."

"I know," Eve said, quietly now, a scolded child.

He looked at her reflection in the mirror and said, "Eve, you
know about the baby Pari is about to have. I'm going to name him
Blue."

She stared at him, uncomprehending.

"Before she came to Italy, before that night—I had thought—I wanted to get you a present when we came back to the city. It had to be blue because it was your favorite color. Do you remember telling me that?"

Eve nodded. A tangle of words between them.

He continued, "I thought I would buy you a piece of jewelry or a ribbon for your canvas rolls. I thought a gift could say more than I ever could, but it never seemed like enough. Perhaps I should have done it anyway, no matter how—" There were tiny lines, fissures over the surface of her porcelain face that seemed to widen as though threatening to crack open, making him think that he had once again managed to screw things up. He had only meant to acknowledge a past possibility, to let her know those days with her in Florence had saved him, but his gesture was too large and absurd. He couldn't take it back now. He resisted an urge to shiver.

"I don't have a favorite color," she said, her voice cold, but he detected on its edge a slight trembling. "I don't remember having said something so idiotic."

She left him there, in front of the vanity mirror—a middle-aged man, staring at the lines on his palm. Even the humiliation he felt couldn't rob him of that discovery—she remembered. He had not imagined those large brown eyes, which refused to meet his now but had once held him with regard, with tenderness. *Blue, Blue,* he felt the word in his mouth, at the back of his tongue, the inside of his cheeks. There was no question that would be the name of his child. He felt that ethereal certainty as though in some other time, in another cosmos where the constellations were off-kilter, unrecognizable to him, having been arranged by a different god, he had already done so, whispered *Blue,* called his child to him.

♦

On Eve's twenty-eighth birthday, seven years before, she and Pari drove up to the Adirondacks to celebrate. Pari had rented the house for the weekend, one with a lake front where she'd hoped they could take freezing dips and amuse themselves, but it snowed the entire drive and once they got there, Pari saw the lake was frozen. She had asked if there was anyone else she should invite, but like usual, Eve shook her head. Over the years, there had been one or two men Eve had expressed interest in, but Pari would watch the brief relationships dissolve without any explanation, not even the hint of a quarrel. Once, Pari called a man Eve had been dating for a few months and pretended to ask him to come to an art gallery opening with her and Eve. On the phone, he hesitated and then admitted that it wasn't possible for him to continue seeing Eve. He remained vague, circled the conversation without answering Pari's questions. Still she persisted in pushing him to confide in her. *It's difficult to explain. She's not bad to look at, talented, but—making love to her is like doing it with a corpse. She isn't there. Actually, she's like that with most other things too. It gives me chills to think. . . . I don't like to feel that way.* What way? Pari pressed. *Like rape. Like I was a rapist.*

Outside, snowflakes crisscrossed diagonally in the air, thickly piling on the house's porch, the lake's frozen surface. Pari thought about one person, the only one who didn't seem to find Eve disconcerting, who had spent weeks with her in Florence before Pari came, whom she wanted to marry someday and who many years later still refused to tell her what had happened between him and Eve. Quickly she shrugged off the thought and its accompanying guilt. It was fine, even flattering that Eve had no one else but Pari, cared about little else but painting, and even then only painting Pari.

Eve seemed to be in a better mood than usual. Together, they ate canned spaghetti and finished two bottles of wine.

"Congratulations," one said.

"Congratulations to you as well," the other echoed.

For two young women in their late twenties, they had achieved everything others only dreamed of, their lives completely entwined. One name was never mentioned without the other. Pari still mused with satisfaction about their college classmates, who she knew had thought her as nothing but a face on the wall. But she was more, much more; she was the one Eve chose. She knew that now.

On the third bottle, Eve picked up her glass and went outside to the porch. Pari noticed she had not put on shoes. Through the glass window, Pari looked at gusts of wind beating the side of her friend's body so violently that she was afraid they would knock her over or, worse, carry her off. What would happen to Pari if Eve disappeared? The thought was intolerable. Pari's identity had grown dependent on that dark shape on the other side of the glass. Perhaps another kind of life was possible, but it wouldn't be vital or worthy.

Before she could join Eve, she called out and demanded that Eve at least put on boots and a coat; Eve turned toward the window and retched continuous gushes of undigested wine. Small clumps of red speckled the white blanket at her feet. When she was done, she lifted her eyes and grinned at Pari, a glimmer of undiluted innocence in her expression. Pari couldn't move, afraid she was for Eve, of Eve—in the snowstorm, her unhappiness so glaring it threatened to swallow them both.

In the morning, they attempted to take a stroll over the lake's frozen surface. Eve was peeling a boiled egg as she walked, crunching snow underfoot and singing the happy birthday song to herself. Pari was by her side. If someone saw the two women, he might think, *How pleasant they seemed, how intimate they looked.* Overnight the ice had thinned; Pari moved cautiously, as though she could control the amount of weight exerted in each of her steps. She was nervous but glad about an email she had received earlier—once again, all of Eve's paintings had sold out and *Vogue* had reached out to Pari about featuring a profile of the two of them. Pari related the news, careful not to sound overly excited.

"For the photo shoot, they might want to dress us up a bit□— you know, a magazine like that, they have their own vision," Pari said, eyeing Eve's maroon dress, one identical to the seven that she owned.

"Dress up how?"

"I know how it sounds, but they'll make us look good together."

"Good?" Eve said.

"Seductive."

"It's just a way of undermining my work," Eve said. "The cheapest kind of intrigue."

"Why not use it to our advantage?" Pari tried not to show her frustration. Without her, Eve wouldn't be enjoying the accolades they now had. She probably wouldn't have been able to make a living. She had always needed Pari to nudge her in the right direction.

"Do it without me."

"What are you talking about?" Pari frowned. "They want us together. It's an article about *us*. Don't you get it?"

Ahead of them, pine trees encircled the lake's edge. Beneath Pari, the ice began to feel like sponge. She grabbed Eve's wrist.

"I was thinking—I think that it's about time I move on to something else," Eve said, trying to free herself from Pari's grip. But Pari's fingers only seemed to tighten around Eve's pulse.

"Move on? Move on with what? What are you saying exactly?"

With the other hand, Eve pulled a roll of papers from her jacket's pocket. "I'm applying for jobs."

"You have a job. Your job is to paint." Pari grimaced. "I'll take care of everything else. Eve, you're doing this backward—artists wait tables so that they can afford to make art, not the other way around. I've always taken care of you, of us. Look at everything you have! What would you be like without me?"

"I don't have a job!" Eve shouted. "I have a problem. I've drawn you for nine years. Just you. I can't do it anymore."

"So what are you going to do?" Pari laughed. "Wait tables? Work in an office? Who would hire you? Nobody can stand being around you. You wouldn't last a day in those environments. I'm the only one for you."

"I know," Eve said. She hurried ahead, away from Pari. Then the frost beneath her caved and she stumbled like a puppet for a moment before falling in. Pari immediately stepped back from the hole that seemed to draw more and more ice into its gaping dark. She watched as Eve thrashed about in the freezing water.

"I can't swim. Please!" Eve reached and grabbed at the air. Her pupils bulged out of their sockets like a dying fish's.

"Tell me you're not going to quit," Pari said with measured calm. "Say you're not going to give up painting."

Eve held onto a ragged chunk of ice and tried to pull herself up, but she did not have the strength and slipped back down. "I can't feel my legs," she begged while Pari softly repeated, *Say it. Promise me.* Words floated from her lips like individual globules of fog. Pari found a thick tree branch nearby and showed it to Eve, who nodded and spoke with water in her mouth. "I won't. Stop. Paint . . ."

The two silhouettes were alone in that mute and frozen landscape. If anyone had spotted them from a distance, they might think, *How lucky was the drowning girl, how fortunate her friend was there to save her.*

Pari's hands quivered violently. Her insides felt like rocks breaking along a fault—an earthquake across her body. She leaned on the kitchen sink to steady herself. Eve was soaking in a lukewarm bath while Pari boiled more bottled water, as the house's pipes were frozen, to add to the tub. She regretted her cruelty, how she'd hazarded Eve's life, but Pari believed she had done only what was necessary. It wasn't vain of her to see what Eve couldn't, that together the two of them had a chance at *meaning*, even if such meaning compelled the death of stars, their crashing into earth—an irrecoverable cataclysm. Without each other, they were nothing but leftover dust, kicked up from the history of braver lives.

Pari pushed open the bathroom door, asked, "Have you warmed up?" She came in with the kettle. Slowly she poured it into the bath, careful not to scald Eve's skin.

"Hm," Eve sighed.

"I'm sorry I—" Pari started to say.

Eve interrupted, "Don't; I don't know what I was thinking. You were right. I can't run away from the only thing I do well." A thin film dropped over her dark brown eyes, giving her a resigned, vacant look.

Pari smiled, relieved.

Eve continued, "I wonder about the others, those who are given either useless gifts or simply gifts society doesn't tolerate. Like killing."

"They can always join the army."

"Right, a kind of structured murder in the name of whatever available cause . . . but most people would have agreed to punish you if I had died out there."

"Do you think I would deserve punishment?" Pari said.

Eve looked at the ceiling and murmured something Pari couldn't make out. She didn't ask for her friend to repeat herself.

Pari laced her cold fingers in Eve's now warm and supple ones. Pari felt a lucid truth: it didn't matter what either she or Eve individually deserved. It didn't matter at all because what happened to one would inevitably be felt by the other, absorbed like aftershock, which rang so much louder, lasted so much longer than its origin.

Afterwards, Eve crawled into bed and pulled the fluffy comforter to her chin. Without her oversized dress, Pari saw how tiny her friend was, so insignificant Pari could blink her away, if not for the one thing. Pari sighed.

"Will you stay?" Eve asked. "I don't want to sleep alone."

Pari nodded, "Of course."

They were close enough for one to feel the other's body heat. Pari put her arm across Eve's stomach. No matter how things got, Pari thought about nothing else. It was something neither of them would ever admit: their wish to be consumed by the moment.

"I'll do the photoshoot," Eve said, "but I'm not going to dress up."

"I'll talk to them," Pari said.

"Thank you."

Pari kissed Eve's head, "Don't be silly."

"Pari, I've got an idea for a new series, for our next show—"

Pari smiled, "Of course you do. What is it?"

"You as weather. . . . I can begin with ice. I would sketch tomorrow, but I didn't bring my stuff."

"Your entire studio is in the car trunk, don't worry."

"Hey," Eve said.

"Yes?"

"In a different reality, who do you think we would be?"

"Maybe you would be a waitress." Pari closed her eyes. "And maybe—"

"Yes?"

Pari thought, *Maybe you and Liam*, but she stopped herself, "Never mind."

"You would be a cat person, maybe?" Eve said.

Pari smiled, "I could definitely have a cat. Yes, a little calico. Yes, yes."

♦

Blue came: the wished-for punishment. Before him, Liam had kept children at a distance, seeing in them humanity's ego, a temporary solution to an ancient fear. Against a well-honed, lifelong belief, he wanted Blue.

♦

Pari sometimes took Blue to Eve's studio. Although Eve hadn't been painting much, Pari made sure to show up even if only to sit on a hard chair while Eve paced from one corner to another, made and remade her coffee, insisting that something tasted off and pouring it down the sink after one sip. Her last exhibition had not gone well, reviewed in a major newspaper by the young man who had challenged her at Pari's wedding. Suddenly people were questioning her talent, asking themselves how she had managed to fool them for so long when her technical skills were lacking. All the marketing Pari had done, which focused on the two friends as a pair, had backfired. The media now treated Eve not as an artist but as a psychopath who had achieved wealth and fame from sucking the soul out of her singular subject, her one and only friend. The few small groups of people who still endorsed her work worshipped her like she was a cult leader.

The days idled by. Pari worried that Eve would not return to her work anytime soon. Without this source of income, Liam's salary would barely be enough to support the lifestyle she'd gotten used to. Perhaps they would have to leave the city. Her husband had always talked about raising Blue in the countryside, but she couldn't bear the idea. She was somebody here, first the adored friend of an artist and now the victim.

Magazines and book editors contacted Pari promising a generous advance for an insider view of her life with Eve, what it was like to be oppressed. They outlined to her the angles they could use: the abusive relationship between models and photographers or actors and directors, the correlation between mental health and creativity, the crimes only the famous could get away with. She wouldn't even have to write the book, only grace them with a few interviews now and then and allow the cover to bear her name. When she hesitated, they told her that this was her chance to be a role model. *For what?* she'd asked. *A social and political cause*, they answered. *Which one?* she pursued. *Any of them*, they responded. They mentioned nothing about how it would be a huge betrayal to a friend, how it would crush Eve. Pari refused the offers, but the editors' words tugged at her. She believed she'd had free will when she had done what Eve asked of her, but perhaps. . . . Still, it would be dishonest to deny her own craving for the life Eve had brought them. Did that make Pari a victim? Whose fault was it—the addict, the drug, or the unintended consequences of art?

One evening, having sat for six hours in Eve's studio, Pari had a thought that she believed could cheer up Eve and get her to work again.

"Why don't you paint me and Blue?" she said.

Eve was sitting on the kitchen counter, smoking and picking ground coffee from underneath her nails. She stirred, looked up at Pari and then at the bundle of sleep she was rocking in her arms.

"We don't have to do anything with the pictures," Pari continued, worried she would lose Eve's attention again. "Don't worry about selling anything. Just draw like you used to."

Eve blinked slowly, turned her head sideways, but Pari could tell the idea at least didn't upset her. Maybe it even intrigued her.

"Blue—" Eve noised.

"Yes, Blue."

"What if they say I'm exploiting a child . . . ?"

"I'm his mother. Isn't it a sign that I trust you? It might help," Pari said.

"I've never painted anyone besides you. I don't know if I could—"

"You'll try."

Eve nodded.

♦

Even though Liam had heard of the changes that would come with being a father, he had not anticipated the deep well-being that overtook him, the peace that accompanied the knowledge that he was utterly in love with his son. And the affection he felt for Blue extended to the boy's mother. For the first time in his life, he no longer dreamt of dying, instead feared any sign of bodily deterioration or illness that might cut short his earthly time with

Blue. He stopped questioning the rigid structure of work and weekends; the long hours he spent at his desk were not self-serving but necessary for Blue to not want for anything. Every action he took had a new gloss of meaning.

As Liam aged, he became more content because that meant Blue was growing older too. His son held him spellbound with his love of running and his speed (even though he was only four and often stumbled), his preference for orange-colored food, his innocent questions that forced Liam to examine his life and scrutinize his answers so as to teach Blue gently and not corrupt him too soon with adult knowledge. He was pleased at seeing that though Blue needed his mother, he preferred Liam, and laughed more in his company. Perhaps he should have been troubled at the way Blue treaded on eggshells around Pari as though he couldn't quite tell what she would be like from one moment to the next, but he didn't pay much attention to his wife, hadn't looked directly at her in years—in his mind, her face was only ripples of all those reflective fabrics in their bedroom. More often, it was the back of her neck, the lines that framed her ears that he looked at.

He still had nightmares of death, except it was no longer his own, but Blue's. He often forgot about them upon waking or dismissed the images as the mind's illustrations of his worst fears in order to inoculate him against them. Unconsciously, he avoided taking Blue near large bodies of water and got irrationally angry when he learned he was bathed at Eve's studio, and then felt soothed when Pari said Eve had wanted to; it was Eve who had bathed him. Without understanding why, he wanted Eve to love Blue.

In his office hung a painting Eve had given him for Christmas: Blue as a baby holding up ten fingers covered in paint. Different shades of blue were the major tones for all of Eve's paintings of his son, except for the ones that also depicted Pari who was always in lighter pigments, white or pale gray, and either as a figure leaving the frame or so faintly colored it seemed she wasn't there at all.

Changing her major subject hadn't resurrected Eve's career from its free fall, but he was glad she'd found a way to continue painting, selling enough to live barely above destitution; and perhaps that was only due to the fact he had been anonymously purchasing most of her work, which over the years had amounted to hundreds of pieces that he kept in a rented storage unit. She never thanked her unknown patron and never responded to the notes of encouragement he sent along with the money, but once in a while she would send what looked to him like a piece of tile that belonged to a larger mosaic. He had begun to fit them together, but it was still difficult to make out the picture.

♦

That evening in Florence, the one that continued to haunt the three of them: on their third bottle of a local wine, Pari balanced two full glasses on her palms and pretended to be a juggler. When she dropped them, a little deliberately, the dark plum liquid splashed everywhere, on the tiles, his clothes; he laughed and helped her unzip her stained white blouse. He and Pari went on laughing, making little pirouettes on the balcony, she in her lacy flesh-colored bra, he only pretending to hang onto his unbuttoned shirt, both ignoring the fact that they were being watched through the glass door—Eve gripping her pencil, manically sketching. He stole glances at her, her thin wrist that hovered above the drawing pad, her dry lower lip she'd bitten to shreds, the loose yellow dress she wore that only emphasized her evanescing body, her pinched face. He wanted to go to her, bring her a plate of bread, let her refuse to eat it. He wanted to sink in that slow-dark she was surely spiraling under. Still, that unwavering, unforgiving gaze kept him rooted where he was, where Pari staggered into his arms. The beautiful girl, her undeniable warmth, and the damning pain in his chest that hinted at another life, another trajectory, other sorrows he might have known had he more courage.

He breathed in the scent of Pari's hair, its pineapple sharpness; took in her lovely features. He didn't stop her when she unhooked his belt, reached her hand down and fondled his balls. Soon, they both would be naked; despite knowing his movements were absorbed, recorded, seared into Eve's corneas and then reproduced on cold, blank pages, he had gone too far and wouldn't stop now. He pushed into Pari, felt the ancient moon collapse, its deafening crash, and when she screamed at him, begged him to stop, her palm pierced by a glass shard, he did not hear her.

Eve,

if she heard Pari's cry over the door,

was silent as glass.

Not a twitch in her expression, only a continuous gaze—wide and unblinking, faithful only to the page.

♦

To afford another month's rent, Eve had sold most of her possessions, paintings, limited prints; auctioned off her used palette, wrinkled sketches from her early phase as an artist. Her studio apartment was mostly empty except for a large print above her bed: a *Vogue* spread of her and Pari, Pari looking outward, her face ringed by light, pale and cool as the moon. Everything else was submerged in a silky black. Eve was turned toward Pari, barely discernible from the mute darkness, her hand holding a paintbrush and at the same time smearing Pari's eye shadow so that Eve's colorful fingerprints dotted her friend's cheekbone. The photo shoot had been comical, making Eve look more like a makeup artist than a painter. Still there was something honest about the photograph that she liked, the way neither of them resisted shadow or light, the half designated for them.

Eve leaned against the headboard as she chewed on a fist-sized piece of bread that had hardened almost to stone. Time had stilled her if not resigned her to the idea that there weren't other truths to be gained; her relationship with Pari had monumentalized Eve's work in the art world even as it eventually left her destitute. A life could only bear so much significance before imploding into madness. Eve's bondage to Pari—like a car crash that infected the survivor, robbed of loved ones, with a boundless grief and at the same time granting a glimpse of an exquisite knowledge in that momentary brush with death. Eve stopped chewing, letting the dry bread adhere to the roof of her mouth, and closed her eyes.

In her mind, she reached for another life, a gentler outcome, but even with her overactive imagination she couldn't conjure a single picture. *This is the way it must be. The only way.* She watched a cockroach scurry across the tiles—it seemed to be going somewhere with purpose. Eve might never leave her bed again, never go through another door, her wish for change throbbing on its last pulse. She allowed herself a warm tear: such loss, such godly pain were gifts only the lucky few would have. There wasn't room for anything else.

♦

One evening, in the dim light of their apartment, Liam and Pari stared at the TV, listened to its loud blast of voices—a nightly ritual. Without looking at his wife, he recounted his day, his conversation with his boss, the large bonus he could expect by the end of the year. Perhaps it was time to look at a larger apartment, he suggested.

"Somewhere we can permanently settle," he said, proud that he was able to offer this, not an easy task in this expensive city.

"A three-bedroom brownstone," Pari joked.

He smiled. "Maybe not a brownstone, but a two bedroom isn't unrealistic. Blue will need his own room eventually."

"Eve hasn't been paying her rent. She'll get kicked out soon," Pari said. "She's talking about leaving the city."

"Where would she go?" he asked, wondering if the money he sent had not been enough after all.

"That's not the point. Don't you see?" she said. "She can't leave. We can't let her. What would I do without her?"

"What do you want to do?" What he really wanted to say was that Pari had plenty of offers and opportunities; she would be fine without Eve. But perhaps he hadn't understood his wife as well as he assumed.

"We should help her," she said. "We can help her find a new place eventually. In the meantime, can she stay with us?"

He frowned, wondering if this was a test. "Stay with us," he repeated.

Pari nodded. "Eve is proud. She would never ask, but I think I can get her to accept."

Of course, he feared what such a living situation, such close proximity, would lead to, but he was confounded by his wife's generosity. He knew he had underestimated her, though in what ways he had yet to understand. For now, it was best not to act too

alarmed and give away the fact that the idea of being able to financially provide for two women had an enormous appeal to his ego.
Liam restrained himself from asking further questions.

He nodded then. "I'm fine with it if you are."

That night, he held Pari to his chest as he fell asleep, something he hadn't done in a while. He felt grateful to her without
quite understanding why. For the first time in years, he had little
idea what the future would look like, yet this uncertainty did not
upset him, someone who had grown dependent on routines and
predictabilities. In the blank darkness, he smiled to himself. Such
tiny hope was not dangerous, his drifting consciousness assured
him, though he didn't know exactly what he was hoping for.

Eve moved in the following week. He had sold the sofa and purchased a pullout couch in preparation. Without telling Pari, he
had gone to several department stores, walked up and down the
aisles, perusing bed sheets and pillowcases. He wanted Eve to find
comfort when she put her hand on the cotton; he wanted to con-
vey that she could stay as long as she liked.

Every morning, he was disappointed to see that she hadn't
pulled out the sofa into a bed, had slept directly on the cushions,
and the new sheets he bought remained sealed. It wasn't until the
fifth day that she even opened the duffel bag she'd brought with
her, took from it her own towel, and showered. He felt sorry that
he was obliged to leave, to stay away all day long, knowing Eve was
there amongst the items he had chosen, purchased, used time and
time again, extensions of him. One evening, he went home, knowing Pari would be out picking up Blue from daycare. He found
Eve resting her head on the kitchen's granite counter.

He touched her shoulder gently so not to startle her. She stirred,
smiled a smile of sleep.

"Eve, I'm glad you're here," he said.

"I wasn't really in a position to refuse."

"You're not a burden," he said. "I just want you to know that."

"Will you sit for me?" she asked, moving toward the living room. Eve gestured for him to sit on the sofa where she'd slept. She sat down on the opposite chair and picked up her drawing pad with an unguarded anticipation on her face. He half-chuckled, cleared his throat, and sank into the cushions, which released a feminine must that slightly hardened his cock.

He wished for something clever to say, something funny, to disguise his discomfort—he remembered the last time Eve drew him. He had never seen those drawings, but surely he must have looked better then than now; his gray chest hair had outgrown the dark ones so fully that he no longer cared to pluck them. He had wanted to die young, and now thought how vain the act would be: a defense against the ticking clock, a complete halt against earthly decay. It must have crossed the mind of every young suicide, their youth entombed in the memories of those who knew them. Saved from the indignity of aging.

Yet it was perhaps the bravest thing anyone could do: allow time to take its course.

It was the most peace he'd felt in a long time, watching Eve work. She didn't try to fill the silence, her concentration private, otherworldly. Her minimal style, as he remembered from Florence, had gone, occupied by deep trembling lines as though the act of drawing was too much for her, and yet her shading was light and swift—expressions of ease and experience. She was completely at home when she worked. Seeing his image materialize under her fingertips, he understood why Pari had been captivated for so many years. Every time he glanced at the work and thought it finished, Eve surprised him by adding layer on top of layer, spiraling the portrait from itself, submerging it with unusual geometric shapes. It wasn't exactly how he saw himself, but perhaps how Eve would be inside him. Hours passed.

"You're sweating," Eve said.

He was jolted from his thoughts. "Ah, yes."

Eve smiled, her face wide open and innocent. Liam could tell the work had energized her.

"Sketching you was a pleasure," Eve said.

Liam reddened. "We can—I can anytime you like."

"You know, I've been working with Pari for so long, I thought anyone else would be impossible—but she is inside you, too. And Blue. Perhaps this is why."

In front of the mirror, Pari dabbed pearls of cream underneath her eyes. "Am I not beautiful anymore?"

He laughed and said, "I'm going to bed." He left her there, alone with her reflection.

That night, he was startled to turn and find his wife next to him. She'd come in so quietly and lay down without a sound. In the dark, he always found it easier to be kind to her.

"Don't worry so much," he started. "Half of the women in this city still envy you."

"And you? What do you think of me?"

"I won't ever leave you or Blue. Not for anything."

"Staying with me isn't the same as loving me," she said.

"I won't leave," he repeated. It was the most he could offer. Between Liam and Pari, they had not pretended that their relationship was anything beyond the ordinary. Love was perhaps the least of their concern. The blunt honesty of their partnership had worked; why was she suddenly wanting more?

When he woke in the middle of sleep, as he normally did, and went to the bathroom, he saw Pari already there leaning over the sink as Eve cut off chunks of his wife's hair, the wet locks in the white washbasin like tangles of tree roots. They didn't blink when he turned on the lights, didn't acknowledge him, as though he were a sleepwalker wandering into the wrong dream. Their mutual silence embarrassed him, but he must carry on what he came in to do so pissed in the toilet. He stood there for what felt like an interminable length of time—his soft penis shrunken to a mortifying size in his hand—before managing to push the liquid from his body. Even then the stream came out slowly and painfully.

In the morning, he reached out to touch Pari's head, shocked when his palm grasped at the empty air and then the choppiness near her scalp.

"Whose idea was it?" he asked, trying not to show irritation.

"Mine."

"Really?"

"Eve helped."

"And Eve didn't question why you would want to ridicule yourself like this? What about work? You said you would consider that hair commercial—now what?"

Pari shrugged. "I've got Eve."

"I'll take Blue today," he said, worrying about what the teachers and the other parents might think if they saw his wife. "Please go get a proper haircut. Shave it all off if you must. Get a fucking wig."

He hurried off then, taking Blue without giving him his breakfast. As soon as he shut the door, he wondered if he had heard a burst of laughter from the inside, and stood for a moment listening, then decided that he must have imagined it. He didn't know then, couldn't anticipate the magnificence of female solidarity, its determination to bring him to his knees.

♦

Squares of mosaic continued to arrive, quicker than they had before. Liam kept them in a box in his office, awaiting the time when no other would come. Then, only then, would he go to the storage where he had already begun gluing the earlier tiles onto the walls, the hint of a picture slowly emerging. He wanted to assemble the whole thing then.

That decision would cost him, *the first mistake in a series of mistakes to follow*, but such was the thing with little errors: they seemed inconsequential, undetectable; their destructive potential lay in their ability to accumulate.

♦

He had pictured it differently: soft afternoons, short and fulfilling exchanges, a question or two. What did Eve think of a movie, a color? What did she really feel about fruits dipped in chocolate? These small pleasures he thought he might have without disturbing the structure of his life, Pari still rubbing lotion on her legs in the bedroom, Blue asking impossible questions. For a while, it lasted.

He was convinced of the household tranquility, thankful that his wife never asked why he didn't come back to bed after waking in the middle of the night. He wanted Eve's friendship, that was all. She was always awake when he came—in fact, he had never seen her sleeping. He whispered mundane words, told himself it was because he didn't want to wake Blue. In the night's silence, he offered nothing but his loneliness, his burden. He was careful not to reveal any dissatisfaction with his marriage. It wasn't wrong to share a few blueberries with his houseguest, giving her only the round, plump ones he had carefully picked out, watching her bite the already tiny fruits in half. One night, he turned the white glare of his laptop's screen toward Eve, demanded she look at several properties he was considering. He scrolled through pictures of two-bedroom units, then changed the filter option to three. He looked at Eve then, asking without asking, afraid of his own audacity.

"What do you think. Do you like this place," he said.

"I like that oval window."

"Can you picture yourself there, under your very own window." He deliberately made this sound like a comment instead of a question.

When she didn't respond, he asked, "Eve?" He closed his laptop, turned to her.

"I'm at a house in the country," Eve breathed, her eyes closed. "The floorboards feel damp. There's a blue-winged moth on the kitchen counter; it has frozen to death, but its color is still bright. I go upstairs to my studio, where there is a large window. From there, I can see the trees, the skyline, a lake in the distance." Abruptly, she opened her eyes, stared into his, "That's where I should be."

He smiled, moved by her idyllic imagination, "Who are you there with?"

She shook her head. "I'm alone in my studio. I think—I think there is a child outside, a little boy. He never speaks, and I never talk to him. He walks toward the lake and I'm screaming from my window, but he can't hear me. It's just a recurring dream I have."

"I have those too," he said.

She shook her head again as though he hadn't understood, as though he couldn't possibly. "It's the only dream I have."

"Eve, I know Pari enjoys having you here," he said. "And Blue adores you. I'm not saying you should live with us for good, but would it be so strange if you did? Not in this little apartment, of course, but I'm looking for something better." He gave this prepared speech while staring at the creases on his palm as though they were maps to his future, not daring to look directly at Eve. When he turned again to face her, her head was on her pillow, her pupils oscillating underneath her lids, her knees to her chest—dreaming her only dream.

She was wearing the same maroon dress she had worn at his wedding, which covered up her entire body, leaving only the ankles exposed. He stared at her sleeping body, her falling and rising chest, and tried to imagine the thin flesh underneath. He wondered about the color of her nipples, if they were a dark brown like Pari's, or crimson, or so pale they merged with the rest of her skin. His mouth watered at the thought of taking one in, rolling it over and under his tongue, his taste buds soaking up its particular saltiness, its discrete fragrance.

He hovered his hands over her head and began to trace the air around her silhouette. His fingers reached the little bit of exposed skin around her ankles and he let his hand gently fall there. She stirred slightly but did not wake. With his pinkie, he lifted the dress's hem slightly, fingered the goose bumps that blossomed on her leg. Encouraged by her stillness, he grazed his hand up her calf, behind her knees, then abruptly, he yanked his hand away, disgusted at what he might do had there been no consequence. The pain of his lust throbbed on the tips of his fingers. In his panic, he wondered if this was how a rapist might feel, moments before yielding to his own brutality. A desire so volcanic—and afterward, the tranquility.

Quickly he glanced at the door of the bedroom and noted with enormous relief that it was closed—Pari sleeping, and Blue as well in the small, adjacent room, which was more like a closet. He cursed such a situation, then questioned if his desire for Eve required the fact of his wife being a few feet away, if the strength of his emotions relied on the very circumscriptions of his life; every love necessitated specific occurrences, and only very lucky people were free to pursue their yearning.

He stood up, reached down his underwear to readjust his erect cock and strap it in place under the waistband of his sweatpants. He would not jerk off tonight, unwilling to acknowledge that the life he fell into was not the one he wanted, even more unwilling to fulfill his primal appetite the way he had once done as a younger man—its punishing, humiliating ache something he now welcomed.

Under the sheets, chilled from the night air that hissed through the cracks in the walls and vents, Pari slept without dreams, without rest, her life having always been anchored by the construct others created, the reality of the willful. Her ears, unable to close, had absorbed the sound of whispers from the living room, their intimacy, fragments impossible not to assign meaning to. When Pari woke, her joints ached as though she'd accidentally slept a thousand nights, her heart a dull thudding in her chest. She went to the bathroom, and for the first time in her life, didn't check herself in the mirror, her reflection suddenly only a distant interest.

She told her husband to take care of Blue, or to ask Eve to. Pari was exhausted—the familiar sense of relinquishment she'd felt seven years before when she'd checked herself into a women's wellness center. Back then, she'd explained to Liam that she was simply tired and needed a supervised break. Pari herself didn't want to admit how frayed her mind had become—the pressure to perform, to keep up her appearance, the spotlight that was never quite bright enough. At the center, she'd regained weight she'd worked hard to keep off for modeling, dyed her hair an ugly purple because it matched the evening sky, yelled profanities whenever it suited her to do so, danced every day at noon as part of a movement therapy session, even made friends—it was wonderful. Perhaps it should be a mandatory retreat for anyone who lived life head-on, ruthlessly. She would never have wanted to leave but for Liam, who diligently visited every three days with board games, magazines, chocolates. She'd been convinced then of his love for her. But perhaps it was his sense of duty. All of it was returning.

"I'm a little tired today," she said.

Liam nodded, shrugged her off with an unfamiliar cheerfulness. She slipped back under the covers; she needed sleep, more sleep, its numbing of all physical truths, its consoling emptiness.

"Eve?" Pari called when she woke for the second time that morning. Or was it many mornings later? It seemed only a few hours had gone by, but it could have been a few days, even months. Her throat was sore and her back ached. When no one answered, she pulled herself up. Apart from the rain that spattered rhythmically on the windows' glass, the house was silent.

"Eve?" Pari said again, suddenly panicked at the thought of being alone. Eve was sitting on the living room floor, painting a palm-sized square of tile. Around her were scattered tubes of color, glue, ropes, dirty tin cans—Pari frowned, annoyed at the transformation of her living room. "Why didn't you answer me?"

"You didn't call," Eve said.

"I did. A few times." Pari sat down, picked up the glue gun, squirted a dot of hot glue on the tip of her finger. Her skin burned but quickly cooled, giving her no time to mention the pain.

"You look terrible," Eve said, without glancing at Pari. "You should have taken Blue to school. He's been asking about you."

"No, he hasn't. He was probably thrilled for you to take him." Pari picked up the rope and began coiling it around her elbow. "Was my husband out here last night?"

"I don't know. I was asleep," Eve responded, dotting the edges of the tile with yellow.

"I heard you talking."

"You must have been dreaming."

"Maybe," Pari said. "You don't know him like I do, Eve. He might pretend to be nice to you, but he isn't—"

"Why are you telling me this?"

"I wish I could teach him a lesson in a way he would remember, but he hasn't paid attention to anything I do for a few years..." Pari didn't want to talk to Eve, but who else was there? She felt as though all her life decisions had been misled, but the momentum to push forward was too seductive to resist. She looped the rope around her neck, pretended to hang herself with her tongue out, lolling. Eve laughed. Pari continued, "I wouldn't even know how to kill myself that way, making a knot—"

Eve pulled the ends of the rope from Pari's hand. "It's not so hard. I know about every knot there is."

Eve proceeded to twist the rope, looping it into itself, making exquisite, complicated knots, then undoing them, naming each as she went along, her hands a moving maze.

"This—the Running Bowline.

This—the Soft Shackle.

Here's the Alpine Butterfly

and the Lighterman's hitch."

Pari listened and watched as the coarse rope danced before her, rapt at its serpent-like charm. Eve demonstrated another: a simple, elegant noose, which she fastened before tossing it on the floor between her and Pari.

"I'll leave once I finish the mosaic," Eve said, dipping a brush in an orange paste.

"I didn't know you were working on one. Where are the other pieces?"

"I don't know, but it's not my concern," Eve said. "My only job is to paint them and send them away."

"How many have you got left to do?" Pari asked.

"Eight."

Pari's head spun from standing up too quickly. She ran her hand through her hair, still shocked at what was no longer there. She felt again that new desperate exhaustion, the need to put her body to rest, detach it from the rest of her. Pari, whose entire life had hinged on a physical presence, her power born out of the corporeal, was fading from herself. Up until then, she had been the victor, hadn't she? She believed so—she had conquered the man who at the start was more interested in her friend. Pari was the lifeline, the inspiration for one of the most exciting contemporary artists in the world; everywhere she looked was confirmation of her success, her importance. Yet she wasn't sure if the things for which she'd felt ownership were really hers. She wanted now to crawl away from her own skin, to punish her husband for staying with her and at the same time neglecting her. Even Blue seemed uninterested in being her son, always preferring his father. She grabbed the length of rope without knowing what it was she planned to do, her movements directed by a deep impulse, a light-hearted wish for new beginnings.

"I'm going to take a nap. Wake me up in an hour," she told Eve.

♦

On the park bench, Eve was sweeping watercolors on Blue's cheeks. Liam watched his son squeal with delight. Pari had been staying in bed more and more often; he worried a little, but other things kept him occupied. And now that Pari was no longer bringing in any income, he took on longer hours.

Even though he knew children naturally took to their caretaker, he was fascinated at the quick bond that had formed between Eve and Blue. It seemed she'd never tire at inventing games for him. Their playing, while innocent, had a seriousness that intimidated him. He never joined in their make-believe world, preferring to watch.

"You are an ocean, and I am you," Eve directed. "What does an ocean do?"

Blue lay down on the grass, rolled and rolled, his eyes shut tight. Eve crawled to him, speaking cheerful gibberish. Blue clasped his arms around her neck and pulled her to him.

"Come here, Blue!" Blue demanded. "Come in the water." He waved his arms and legs. Eve pretended to struggle before sinking her head down to his small body. Blue laughed and squirmed as she tickled his exposed belly.

"What a powerful ocean you are," Eve said, continuing to tickle Blue's neck, feet, between his toes, until his face grew bright red. Liam intervened as he often had to, Eve seemingly unaware of how much a child could bear, herself being rigorously absorbed by the game.

"Come on. We need to head back," he said to the two disappointed faces. Eve took Blue's hands as though they were both schoolchildren. They scowled at him to let him know his interruption was not welcome, his world only an alternative they were forced to return to. He flushed and cleared his throat. "Now." They stood up at the same time and followed behind Liam, chatting energetically in an invented language. Always, he became disoriented after these park excursions and looked up at the sky as though it were painted. He said as though fed up, and without turning back to look at them, "Enough. We're not playing anymore," but he couldn't help the smile spreading across his face.

♦

Another night. Another day.

Pari opened her eyes, wondered again with panic if she were alone. Her back was sticky with sweat and a sour odor escaped from the orifices on her body every time she shifted on the mattress. It took her a while to adjust from sleep, to notice in the corner of her bedroom a rippling of fabric. Eve was there, crouched on the floor with her sketchbook.

"What are you drawing?" Pari asked.

"You, my dear, as always," Eve said with a slight sneer.

"Can I see it?"

Eve stood up and came closer to the bed. "Are you sure you want to see?"

"You—you should have let me know you were working. I can get dressed." Pari grabbed the notebook. "This isn't me. I don't look like that. She stared at the creature on the page, its lashless eyes, its gaunt wrist reaching for something invisible, its nails jaundiced and sickly long. "What kind of a joke is this?" She ripped out the picture, balled it up, and tossed it at Eve's feet.

That isn't me, Pari repeated again to herself, but when she looked at her wrists, the thick, bulging veins underneath, nausea rolled upward from her stomach to her open mouth. She got up and ran to the bathroom just in time. Standing at the sink in front of the mirror to rinse her mouth, she didn't dare look at her reflection. *I'll leave the house tomorrow, I'll go out, I will*, she told herself, knowing she had made that promise yesterday, the day before, and the one before that.

"Eve?" Pari said, venturing a few steps into the living room, but found it too bright—the light there stabbing at her corneas, her skin. She stood in the dark hallway and waited for Eve to appear with a breakfast tray.

"You don't need to come out. I'll bring you everything you need," Eve said, walking past Pari to the bedroom. Pari followed.

Pari sat back down on the mattress, relieved at the familiarity she felt there, grateful for her friend's company. Eve handed Pari the cup noodles, which she grimaced at, but took the tea with sugar and honey.

"Tomorrow, can we go to the park? I'd like to take a walk," Pari said, closing her eyes. She wanted to see her husband, longed for the idea of him, yet every night when he came home from work, she would turn her face to the wall and pretend to be asleep. She felt as long as she didn't speak to him, the reality of their life could be kept at bay.

"Of course. We can do anything you like," Eve said, grabbing the teacup before Pari could take another sip. "We can take the train to the beach and walk on the sand."

"I'm tired," Pari said, slowing sinking back into the mattress. "Eve, I'm sorry."

"What for?"

"You've had to do everything—cook, clean, care for Blue." Pari trembled. "My husband doesn't care about what's happening to me. And now, now we've resorted to your drawing me in this state. Hey—"

"Yes?"

"Maybe we should play a prank on him. Tell him I'm dying."

"That would be a good way to punish him. If you were to actually—" Eve said. "But it's no fun if you're not actually here to watch him suffer, is it?"

"He would suffer, wouldn't he?" Pari asked, relishing the thought.

"He would."

Pari smiled. She hadn't realized before that she still had a way to influence her husband, one last card to play. For a moment, she was too focused on imagining this final possibility to notice that her friend was smiling too—the pasted, chalk-white smile of a mime.

"Am I still your favorite subject?" Pari asked.

"Until death do us part," Eve said.

◆

The marionettes dangled from Blue's hands, lifting and dropping their heads as he commanded, now twirling in the air like tiny ballerinas, now folding themselves in half to fit into a box. The dolls Eve knitted had become his favorite toys; one wore a long, patchy maroon dress, the other a multicolored gown made of bird quills.

Sometimes Blue had the urge to pluck the feathers—the sight of them on the marionette, separate from the birds he saw on the streets, upset him. Eve took the feathered doll and demonstrated how to make it laugh, tilting the doll's chin up and down, trembling its shoulders. Blue watched her, mesmerized.

Blue looked up and noticed a lanky figure in the far corner of the room. His mother was watching him and Eve. Her body movements were slack, her arms swinging wildly. As she came toward them, Blue inched closer to Eve.

Pari took the maroon marionette from Blue's hand. She shook its strings ungraciously and without any specific purpose, so that the puppet looked like an inanimate object instead of the lively miniature human Eve had often transformed it into. Blue grew more and more distressed.

"Give her back," he told Pari.

She ignored him and continued to play with the doll. "Which one do you prefer, Blue? This ugly one or the other one?"

"She's not ugly," Blue said, rebellious.

Pari smirked. "How could you say that, son? Do you not have eyes? Look at her. She is hideous."

By this point, Eve had put down the other puppet and gathered it in a heap of feathers in her lap. Pari flipped her doll over and pulled on its leg until the seams ripped, exposing the stuffing: indigo-colored cottons. Blue screamed. For reasons unknown to him, he had always loved the maroon marionette and even more so now that he saw that her insides were blue, which he imagined was the same color as his blood.

"No!" he yelled at his mother and lunged forward to grab the marionette. "IHATEYOU."

Pari didn't resist. Without thinking, she fingered her chest as though Blue's words had been scored there. Her face seemed to close as though suddenly exhausted. She stood up and dropped the marionette, which landed with its legs folded underneath so that it appeared to be sitting, hands on lap. A tiny calm in a roomful of restless fury.

♦

Pari might have been in the depth of sleep, the depth of dreams when she asked, *Eve, what happened between you and my husband in Florence?*

In dreams, in sleep, she dared ask.

♦

Liam didn't give much thought to offering Eve his elbow, which she shyly took as they both crossed the streets of Florence. There were not many cars, so the gesture seemed needless and a little absurd. When they reached the bridge, she still didn't let go of his arm. The whole day they walked together like newlyweds, their pace relaxed. He looked at nothing and everything, a bird's nest atop the branches, an abandoned shoe, a single cloud that seemed to drift along in sync with his every step. His happiness felt so assured that he kept reminding himself they were strangers, as though, because of the fact, he didn't deserve it. He wondered who she was, this girl that aroused no lust in him, numbed his masculine compulsion, and drugged him into a pale, blue-like calm, a waveless serenity. He wanted to stay hypnotized, forever crossing empty streets, forever under the single white cloud.

They stopped at a gelato shop and each got a cone of three flavors. Then they both ate the ice cream in under two minutes. He wanted to lick off the pistachio stain on her cheeks the way a cheerful puppy might but instead said nothing and let her wear the sugary smudge for the rest of the night. He was delighted every time he turned and saw the cream smear on her face. He told himself he would speak no word of promise, of love, though that was what it felt like. Despite his happiness, he was afraid of disturbing the scenery with his confession, his vulnerability.

He spoke of other things: the pungent flavor of anchovies, about music, the pope. Surprisingly, Eve did not know much about worldly topics, but her intuition enabled her to carry any conversation while he always felt the need to cite facts. He got to know her in a slanted way without asking direct questions. In talking about justice, he saw that Eve exhibited a moral coldness that commonly belonged to a general or a judge, someone who frequently made decisions for the life and death of others. He learned her tastes when he commented on the architecture of Italian churches, which she deemed too warm, preferring the isolation of English cathedrals and the cooler tones in German design. There was one subject she was an expert in—her relationship to her own art—but with this she was careful to reveal little.

Every day after that first day, he would again offer her his elbow at the first intersection and, quietly, she would take it. The two of them did little, only walked, looking at nothing.

Even if he wanted to finally admit to his wife that something, indeed a significant something, had occurred before she came between him and Eve, even if he meant to be honest, he wouldn't be able to name this *nothing*, an ungraspable, intangible knot at the furthest reach of his being. How would he even begin to describe this light brush of sunburst—an instance of rare warmth that in the end he had turned from?

◆

"Why?" Blue asked him.

Blue at seventeen was already tall and broad-shouldered as Liam had once been. But unlike him, Blue did not exude arrogance, or even simulated confidence. It grieved him to see his son always hunchbacked, reducing himself wherever he happened to be standing. Some part of him had known that such a question was inevitable, that one day Blue would demand answers to *why* his wife, his son's mother, had killed herself, yet he found himself entirely unprepared. He had taken Blue camping with the hope that the trip would bridge the increasing distance between them lately. Blue was standing with his back to him, pretending to be interested in a blueberry bush. Blue was all that he had. The only beauty in his mismanaged life.

"Why what?" He feigned ignorance, hoping Blue would be unable to verbalize the question he had been dreading for years.

"Why did she do it?"

"She was unhappy," he sighed.

"What was she unhappy about?"

"I don't know."

"How could you not know? You were supposed to love her."

"I don't know."

"Was it your fault?"

He should have shaken Blue, punched him—not like a father would a son, but as one man would another. Instead, he said, "It could have been."

That night, they built a fire together. Blue wouldn't stop stoking it, even after the flames had reached several feet high. Liam worried about the embers floating off into the trees and causing a forest fire but said nothing. Blue circled the pit, cracking branches and feeding the flames. When Blue finally sat down on a boulder drenched in sweat, Liam handed him a beer. Blue took it unceremoniously, but he noticed his son's expression softened. After a few more beers and several hot dogs neither of them bothered to roast, he told Blue that he loved him, something he hadn't said in a long time, knowing it would embarrass him.

"Why don't you remarry?" Blue said. "You're still young enough."

Liam laughed. This son of his was practicing generosity.

"I'm not fit for that stuff," he said.

"Companionship? Love?"

It was strange to be challenged by a boy of seventeen, his boy. It was comforting too to know that someone still cared what he thought.

"Love—" he said, teetering on that easy confessional state alcohol tended to induce, "isn't as noble as you think. Sometimes your love is a burden to another. Better not." As soon as he said those words, he immediately wanted to retract them. He still wished Blue to find a kind of happiness, one he was unable to incite. "Actually, don't listen to me."

"Okay," Blue said. Just like that he eased back into his boyish insolence.

He ruffled Blue's hair, stood up.

"Where are you going?" Blue asked.

"The stars—it's been such a long time since I've noticed them." This dark plummet of nothing, these thousand tiny pinpricks of light pulsing on his temples—he felt sure he'd seen them before, in a dream perhaps when he was simultaneously himself and someone else. Just like a lifetime of mistakes he'd already made and would go on making.

◆

Pari played with the rope Eve had knotted a few months before. She found it this morning under her bed; she couldn't remember if she'd put it there. Had it already been so many days since she'd left the apartment, since Eve helped her shave off her hair? Her husband had expressed anger then, which pleased her, but after that day he no longer spoke to her except out of necessity, as though the weight of dead cells on her head had been the entirety of her identity. Once, he had criticized her for doing nothing but sleep. She had told him then that sleeping was the only thing that made her life with him bearable. She regretted these words immediately, but they were hurled like jagged stones, and he never bothered her again. He left her alone as he thought she wanted. At night, he slept with Blue in the adjacent room.

Pari picked up the dirty spoon that had accompanied the lemon ginger tea Eve had brought in the day before. On the back of it, her reflection—Pari widened her eyes, and the hollow orifice reflected on the spoon widened back at her. She bit her bottom lip and the mirrored image bled. Blood trickled down her chin.

This morning Eve would not bring in a tray of tea and breakfast. As they had discussed, she would bring Pari a chair. Pari stared at the door. Her mind was nowhere, except on that wooden barrier that would open, letting in beams of bluish morning light.

"It's me." Eve came in as planned.

Pari looked at the chair. Eve waited.

"Well?" Pari said.

Eve put the chair on the mattress, beneath the light fixture. Pari looped the rope around her neck as though putting on a piece of jewelry.

"What will you do?" Pari asked. "After—"

"I will go for a walk. I will come back and find you. I will call your husband."

"And a year from today?"

"I will paint what I saw," Eve said.

"Good."

Pari stepped on the chair while Eve steadied it. Pari's hands shook as she reached for the ceiling. She tried to focus on Eve's last painting, what it would show; without a doubt it would restore both their statuses in the art world, which was obsessed with everything posthumous. And her husband—he couldn't imagine this final act of rebellion; courage wasn't a quality he assigned to her. Pari smiled, an unaccountable satisfaction sweeping over her. Books would be written. Films would be made. She would be remembered. For a second her thoughts lingered on Blue, but quickly her worry dimmed. The imagined applause was louder.

"Pari. Are you sure?" Eve said suddenly, disturbing Pari's fantasies. Pari looked down at her friend, whose eyes were moist, who had never asked if she were sure about something before, who had gone along with all her decisions.

"Don't disappoint me now, Eve," Pari said. "If it weren't me, it would be you. It probably was you in some other universe. Or Liam. Either way—"

"It is me too. It is just as well."

Eve slowly withdrew from the bed. Without her keeping it in place, the chair started to wobble. She turned, walked out of the room, and gently closed the door behind her.

In that silent room, you would have to strain to hear—the sound of a chair toppling to its side, the razor-sharp sound of a heavy mass penduluming in midair, held up like a marionette on strings.

◆

Everything looked better from above.

◆

Eve was ahead of Liam, her long shadow still reaching back for him. They came here together, drove up the mountains, walked on damp leaves and dead branches to find this unremarkable field. It seemed too much effort for an expanse of brown weeds and dying trees, yet—

Pari had been dead for twelve days, and Liam needed to keep walking.

There was no one left to stop him from going to her—Eve, whose name he felt he had invented, felt belonged to him—but he was unable to take a step forward. He squinted at the clouds and saw only motes of dust, a thin and impenetrable layer between him and the light. Eve stopped walking, stood suspended in a sunbeam; he knew that she would never turn around to beckon him.

It was Eve who had found Pari hanging from a light fixture;

it was Liam who had taken down the body;

it was his rope, the one he had kept in his suitcase as he traveled around Europe,

then brought back home as a reminder of a choice he had once made—to live;

it was Eve's practiced and elegant noose around his wife's neck;

it was Pari who sent Eve to Florence;

it was Eve he had wanted;

it was Pari's breasts, hair, cunt he had stroked, claimed, and it was the same body that no longer responded to his touch, would stay cold, except for the hair, its unchanging reality bewildering his senses.

He was supposed to grieve but only felt anger, as though an invisible game of chess had been placed underneath his feet and he had been outmaneuvered.

He caught up to Eve. He could strangle her, end her life and his misery; except for the birds, nobody would hear her. She handed him the urn.

"Would you like to do it?" she asked.

He nodded but did not move. "Don't you think she would have wanted someplace more beautiful?"

"There's nothing beautiful about her anymore," Eve said.

"But she was—wasn't she?" He said this as though it somehow explained everything.

Eve nodded.

"Do you have to go? Could you stay? Please stay," he said.

"It's finished." Eve smiled, her eyes looking clouded over as though she were seeing a memory. "There's nothing left for me."

"What about your work?"

Eve shook her head. "I can't. Not without her."

"Where will you go?" he said.

"Somewhere else."

Eve turned and began her walk back. Liam started to weep then—his soul withered, reduced to the weight of the urn in his hands. He called after her, his last attempt.

"Eve!" he shouted. "What about that house you told me about, the one in your dream? Let me help you find it."

"It's a nightmare, not a dream—" she said before turning permanently from him, going rapidly into the distance, farther and farther away until the contour of her diminished, till she was nothing more than a point of pale light.

◆

Liam pushed the final ceramic square in place and stepped back for the first time to examine the result: a culmination of years of his secret admiration for Eve and, in exchange, this art piece she'd created just for him, the only thing he had left of her. Up close, the mosaic was nothing but blurs of colors, gradients of light, shadows upon shadows; but the farther backward he walked, the more the image emerged, as though from his own consciousness, as in an eclipse, a total and engulfing obscurity, then suddenly clarity. It was his own face staring back at him. He laughed, a bitter and exhilarating laughter. She knew, she knew. Eve had always known he was the anonymous patron, and yet she'd never confronted him, never revealed her own secret knowledge. She'd not rejected him, had accepted his adoration from a distance. After a lifetime of dishonesties, lies he'd told others and convinced himself of, this moment of unadulterated truth was more than he deserved. *It's enough.*

CARD THREE

BEING EVE

E ve was five when she became aware of the sky, its separate-
ness and tangibility from herself. Her mother was smoking outside, and the rain, which came down suddenly
in torrents, put out her cigarette. She looked up and cursed the
clouds as though the attack was personal. *Fuck you*, Eve mouthed
to the heavens, imitating her mother. It was then that she also
realized her mother was an autonomous being, distinct and different from her. Eve screamed because there was no other way to
verbalize this frustration, this brutal and psychic severance of a
child from her mother. Eve wept and wept. Her mother couldn't
console her, couldn't understand the sudden outburst. *What is it,
girl?* She carried Eve the whole nine blocks back to their apartment.
The scream spiraled up the stairs, into the living room, behind the
closed door.

"Please, Eve!" Her mother begged. "Tell me what you need."

Her mother paced their tiny rectangular apartment, taking out
toys, objects at random, and waving them in front of Eve. As she
rifled cabinets, she continued to bargain, making promises of ice
cream for dinner, amusement parks on the weekend. Her mother
was frightened that Eve might pass out from exhaustion, her fury
so intense it would stop her heart from beating.

At the bottom of their clothing trunk, her mother searched franti-
cally, automatically, and felt something warm to the touch, something lacy. She pulled it out: the doll, a dirty ceramic figurine,
blinked at her. It must have come with the trunk she inherited
from her grandfather. How long had it been there? She used the
hem of her shirt to wipe dust off its face. Immediately, she marveled at the force of its presence. What doll maker would have
created something like this, a steely perfection—a dead beauty?
Her grandfather, who never married, had once said, *I've not the
pleasure of encountering a beauty which time does not wane.* The doll

must have borne witness to his libertine ways, his unapologetic preoccupation with violating women's trust and their hearts. And perhaps the doll was there too towards the end, its cool ceramic lips drawing in its owner's final gasp of life. She hesitated before bringing it over to Eve, who stretched out her arms and eagerly received it. Immediately she quieted.

Mine, mine.

"So that's all it takes," her mother said, relieved. She slumped into an armchair, lit another cigarette. "Be careful, Eve, it's not a children's toy. That thing will break into a million pieces if you drop it. I won't be able to replace it—it's one of a kind."

Eve clutched the doll tighter. "One of a kind!" She was delighted.

Her mother was grateful to the strange figurine that managed to do the impossible.

"What will you name her?" she asked.

"Par—" Eve started to form a word.

"Par? An odd word, but she is yours to do what you like."

"Pari!" Eve happily shouted.

Her mother laughed, baffled by Eve's imagination. She wished children could explain the secrets only they seemed to have access to—innocence that sounded like wisdom—but she didn't ask Eve how she came up with the name. For now, Eve was content to sit and whisper to Pari, conversations that lasted hours and afforded her mother some time for rest. Tidbits of Eve's words would sometimes reach her mother, their conspired intimacy puzzling her. But like most parents, she dismissed it as nothing but child's play.

♦

Liam touched her cheek with his wrinkled hand, the ridges on his skin fusing with hers. Even with glasses, Eve's vision wasn't quite as good as it used to be, but that didn't matter; after fifty-eight years together, she had memorized every inch of his form. Perhaps she knew him better than he knew himself—just as without him, she would be blind to most of her body. Only last week, he had pointed out a new reddish mole at the base of her neck.

Everything in their house was as old as they were. Sitting in her favorite chair, she asked him to bring her the framed photograph of the two of them when she was in her forties and he in his fifties. He wiped it with the cuff of his sleeve before handing it to her.

"What a fox you are," she joked, thumbing the two figures in the picture.

"Where were we? Must be Thailand," he said, sitting next to her on the arm of the chair.

"I don't look too happy," she said.

"Well, it's fair to be a little grumpy in the middle of, what, a ten-country trip?"

"How remarkable. I can't imagine going beyond the market now."

"It was exhausting," he said. "I prefer us here."

She agreed. "I believe we went because I had another miscarriage."

"That's right," he said. "You decided that we wouldn't try again."

"And we didn't." She smiled. It was nice to be able to say so without feeling the sorrow she'd guarded for so many years.

Upstairs, in her studio, Eve worked on painting a shard of glass—colors ebbing over the reflective surface. She made sure to leave parts of the mirror fragment untouched. When she finished, she held it against the wall, contemplating where to add it on the larger mosaic there. She wondered if she would ever finish, this project that had spanned more than thirty years. It wasn't as though she wasn't grateful, but still, in solitary moments she allowed herself the luxury of imagining what her life would have been like if she had been more successful with her art. Perhaps she should have tried harder.

When she was offered the teaching position upstate, they had fled the city like eager birds migrating south. Back then they were still planning for a family. They had not managed to make a child together; instead, they fed wild birds, shooed away the deer that fed on their garden, looked at hundreds of fireflies curtaining the summer woods. Her husband, if he had other desires, had never let on, never tried to make her feel guilty for the extra hours required of him to supplement her meager salary. Her heart ached from both pity and pride when she watched him in their garage, hunched over the table, sanding the holder he made for her paint-brushes. In such moments, she wondered which one of them was the artist. He'd worked with numbers for most of his life and she'd never asked if he would have preferred finding a career that would make better use of his hands. Sometimes a question was all it took to realize the possibility of a dream. She gripped the tile. Why had she never asked?

"I think the robin's eggs hatched!" His voice reached her from below.

There were moments, pangs of ghostly pain. Their relationship had not been entirely spared by such mischievous gods. Twenty years before, Liam had received a blowjob from a stranger. He told Eve about it that same night. Carefully, she had thanked him for his honesty before asking for the details. *She asked if she could go down on me. I said okay.* He had not apologized, only exacerbated Eve's pain by adding, *That woman was too beautiful to be denied.* Eve retreated to the bathroom, cried alone, cried to her reflection that suddenly seemed inadequate. In the mirror, she saw behind her shoulder the back of a woman's head, her dark hair falling to her small waist—a doll-like perfection. Eve blinked and the figure vanished.

It all seemed so trivial now, comical even that she had considered leaving him—years of right doings measured against one slight. Two years after his confession, she kissed the neighbor out of spite, which she justified as a necessary equipoise to restore their relationship to its former fairness, only to find herself getting drawn further into the kiss, the embrace, the conversation. No, theirs had not been free of errors. Perhaps it was better to let the human tendency to transgress run its course rather than to feed its insidious strength by trying to stifle it. *Even great love needs to be endured.*

Some nights, Eve still thought about the neighbor who had died years ago. She and her husband had attended the funeral together. He was gentle, comforting as she wept, as she wet his shirt with her tears for another man. She knew there was no other who cared more about her, not in this universe or another.

She dropped the glass shard on her desk; it would have to wait till later. She hurried out of the studio, and then paused to look over her shoulder at the mosaic in progress—blue upon blue, shallow water over dark, slices of Eve's own face peeking out from the unpainted parts of the reflective surface and the face she imagined for the girl her husband had met at the bar. Her painting of the girl had taken on many permutations over the years, but the features only emerged from hazy lines and became more detailed after his confession. Her pain subsided as she painted, as she allowed the girl's perpetual youth to merge with Eve's aging reflection. Perhaps in another life, they could have been friends. After all, some similarities in both women had drawn them toward the same man. She would not try to decipher her obsession with the color blue. She smiled to herself, realizing she was past the age of having regrets anymore.

♦

"What are you drawing?"

"Hm—" Eve noised. At sixteen years old, her heart still raced when a stranger spoke to her. He looked older than Eve, but a boy nonetheless. "My doll."

"Aren't you too old for dolls?" The boy moved closer. Perhaps he was flirting in that cruel way teenaged boys did.

"Only one: Pari."

"You can sketch her from memory?" The boy hovered over Eve's drawing pad. "She looks so real."

Eve nodded. Pari was lying safely in her bag, but she wasn't about to tell him that. He sat down on the bench next to her and introduced himself. It was nice to talk to someone when she had been so alone, but she couldn't help herself from immediately scanning the boy's facial features, isolating their flaws, comparing them to Pari's—the ideal face.

Since long ago, the doll had corrupted Eve's imagination. A reverse puppeteer, it was the doll who strung her owner along, propelling Eve on to an impossible search for an equal beauty. She wanted the boy to stay and keep her company but was afraid that like all the boys before he would eventually question her attachment to the doll, that what he had at first found intriguing and wonderful would curdle into something resembling a sickness. Eve thought about telling him to fuck off—that usually worked— but she was suddenly hopeful.

"Do you know anyone beautiful—flawless?" Eve asked.

The boy considered this question seriously, not taking offense. "My mother. But beauty isn't the same as having no flaws."

"Can I meet her?"

Laughing, he said, "Slow down. We should figure out if we like each other before meeting the parents, don't you think?"

Eve joined in his laughter. His lightheartedness was infectious. Together they began walking away from the clamor of the city center toward the narrower, quieter streets—an instinct of fledging love. Inside her bag and against her leg as she walked, Eve felt the doll's ceramic head knock back and forth, its mounting resentment, its insistence on reminding her that it had been just the two of them for years and would always be. People had always found Eve disconcerting, if not outright off-putting. She had become convinced of their view, someone else's reality. Her way of observing—prolonging her gaze a little too long, too directly—appeared to others invasive and even belligerent. Nobody saw it for what it was: a gift, an instinct, for Eve had been an artist long before she made art.

Eve blinked and saw herself in a classroom alone, in the dining hall, at the back of the school bus, on the playground speaking to herself, no longer able to resist the words that had turned acidic behind her sealed lips. Always alone. When the other children stared at her, Eve shoved a handful of sand into her mouth just so she would have a reason to open her lips and let out a stifled scream. The years would stretch on this way uniformly, predictably. It wasn't as if the other children had beaten her or mocked her—Eve cursed herself for not being able to even inspire their animal violence—they simply avoided her, their silence accusing and convicting her of difference. There on her desk sat Pari when she returned from school, always there with its dress fanned in a circle of lace, glad to see Eve. In the third grade she had started taking the doll with her everywhere. For many years it had been a comfort. No one questioned a little girl talking to her doll.

"So, do you draw anything else besides . . . ?" The boy asked.

Eve shook her head.

"It's not a bad thing," he said. "Doing the same thing over and over is the only way to greatness."

"Or madness," Eve said.

"Either is okay with me." The boy looked away as he said this. Eve smiled at his attempt to be agreeable.

Quiet, quiet. Eve tried to will away Pari's voice. She wanted more than anything to grow older, to age, because—adults didn't need dolls, did they? As though reading her mind, the boy suddenly grabbed Eve's hand and pulled her into an alley strewn with ripped tires, torn cardboard, human shadows sucking on glass pipes, burning tiny blue-tinged crystals. Behind a large dumpster, they kissed.

"Want to know a secret?" the boy asked.

Eve nodded.

Around them were other souls just as frightened and desperate for escape—to disappear into another, a kind of love, a way of bargaining for life to be a little more beautiful, a little more bearable.

◆

They wouldn't admit that they were children still and struggled to untangle themselves from the realities they had invented. The boy helped Eve button the back of her dress, a row of pearls that climbed from her lower back up to her neck. They had found the dress at a consignment store. The boy, feeling like a gentleman, had paid six dollars for it. They never knew exactly what game they were playing until they were already deeply mired in it. That day they took the train to the sea.

They walked barefoot for hours on the hot sand, talking about everything, the serious and the playful, wishing to be eternal so they could carry on loving each other and abruptly wishing to die so they would never betray themselves. Looking at Eve in her knee-length ivory dress, her laced collar so much like the one her doll wore, her heels clad with dry sand, the boy made a silent vow. He would always go with Eve, follow her wherever her mind took them—into light or oblivion. This quiet surrendering sent a shiver down his spine and made him chuckle.

They found a shallow cave and lay down to make love. The boy had done this before and Eve had not. At the mouth of the rock wall, she lay with her legs open to the sun. The boy blushed, suddenly embarrassed because he expected her to be more nervous. Eve looked on unblinking at his nakedness as though she were looking at a blank sheet of paper. He positioned himself awkwardly on top of her and slowly found comfort in his own rhythm. Several times he said her name like asking a question to assure himself she was there with him—aside from slowly blinking she did not move. He found it strange at first, then became increasingly aroused at the thought that it was like making love to himself—a natural state of being. When he came, he shut his eyes and hoped that Eve too saw only herself in his pupils and watched as he disappeared.

In the boy's bedroom, they oscillated between worlds, sometimes angrily tossing Lego pieces at each other like children, other times exploring one another's bodies obsessively, clinically, as though their flesh bore a diagram to a higher truth. Once they discovered sensual pleasures, they could not help themselves and made love incessantly, for there were no other indulgences more worthy. And they weren't wrong: as not fully-fledged adults, they were still able to ignore all logic and act solely on their emotions.

While the boy graffitied the ceiling, red fireworks exploding into a sun yolk, the girl sat at the foot of the bed drawing a spider she saw hanging from its web in the room's corner—her first deviation from her doll. They didn't talk about the future because they had no plan, no goal besides being together. Their obstinate love, if anyone had caught a glimpse of it, would laugh in disbelief or shrivel with envy. Maybe they were lucky or maybe they had already paid penance in another life so that now they were content to strive for nothing, achieve nothing, and accept their happiness.

♦

The child had always come to see her, but lately his visits had become more and more frequent. He often appeared after dusk, at the moment she was too tired from the day's burden to resist him. Tonight, he wore blue overalls and stood in that ink-black line between earth and sky as the sun descended.

"Come closer," she beckoned him, "What are you afraid of?"

He grinned, tossed something that rolled toward her feet. A tennis ball.

"Ah, you want to play?" She picked up the ball, readied her hand to throw it back to him. In that instant, she felt a fullness of joy, a well-being she didn't know existed.

"Who are you talking to?" Liam said from behind.

Eve jumped, "Oh, you startled me. I was just—" She put forward her hand to show him, but saw there was no tennis ball there.

She was clutching a handful of damp leaves. "I was just cleaning some dead leaves from the porch," she said in a small voice. A part of her understood that the child must be a mirage, a trick of the mind, but she couldn't help allowing herself this hallucinatory pleasure. She loved him, this son she had not managed to bring into the world.

Many years ago, she had cremated the doll with him, her still-born. It had been her husband's idea as a gesture to keep their son accompanied. *After so long, she has absorbed pieces of you. It would be like having you there with him.* Eve had nodded, smiling at his suggestion, one she couldn't refuse. At a lake near home they had scattered the ashes. The water was clear and still, a mirror of the night sky—a thousand tiny pinpricks of light. When Eve reached down to touch it, the constellations rippled. She felt she could move worlds with just a stir of her finger. How long and patiently her husband, the boy in him, had waited to finally free her—it was so like him to metamorphose a curse into a virtue, the way a sculptor breathed life into a lump of dirt.

◆

Once long ago, a girl and a boy arrived at the underbelly of a bridge. In this labyrinthed city it seemed there weren't any more alleys they hadn't made love in, nowhere left to hide their spent bodies. The boy wasn't a boy any longer but a man, and Eve now a woman capable of seeing herself through eyes that adored the gift others had shunned, fearless eyes that held her with regard and cherished Eve for simply being Eve. She accepted his wish to spend the rest of their life together. He had not changed much, his perpetual boyishness a pliant shield against past and future anguish, his embrace an enclosed circle. *I will do anything to*—a warning of intolerable happiness. It was perhaps this that Eve most needed: a boy's unquestioning devotion to a girl who loved a doll.

◆

After dinner, they walked around the property, a ten-acre piece of land her husband inherited from his father, which was mostly wooded. He was barefoot, so she often called out when he was about to step on cow manure. She had always kept him from making this mistake, although she considered keeping silent this time. It might be a better way to teach a lesson. He was older than she but was often childlike, even more with each passing year.

"What do you want written on your obituary?" she teased.

"That's not very nice of you to ask."

"I'm only being sensible."

"I adore you." He kissed her head. "But don't assume I'll die before you just because I'm older."

She wondered if it was because they didn't have children that he sometimes treated her as though she was his daughter. "It's likely," she said.

"I don't really care to tell others about myself. That's what an obituary is for, isn't it?"

"It's to honor your life."

"Then shouldn't the people attending my funeral already know?"

She pursed her bottom lip. "I only want to understand you better."

"Ah, you mean after an entire life together, you still don't know me at all. I've spent more time with you than with my own parents or anyone else on earth," he said, tilting his head back to face the night sky. "Fine, if I must. The only thing I want on my obituary is that I've loved you, Eve. I've loved you well."

She became silent then. He'd silenced her. She didn't understand how he was still able to surprise her, make her feel like a girl, a girl who went to the market for milk. There, she bought the thing she needed and was happy.

"Our life has been easy," she said. "Even when things have been hard, life has been kind to us. Don't you think so?"

He nodded. "I don't know what we did to deserve it."

They paused at a tree stump and faced each other. For a moment, their gazes were locked—transfixed by something they caught in each other's eyes, an impossible past they had not lived. It held them breathless, this glimpse into another self, another possibility, familiar and out of reach.

◆

"What was the secret?" Eve asked her husband.

He was leaning on the windowsill, his back to her. "I'm not sure what you mean."

"When we first met, you asked if I wanted to know a secret," she said. "But you never told me."

"Isn't it enough to know there is one?"

◆

Dawn came. They had little need for sleep now so followed their habitual pattern out of the bedroom, into their slippers, out to the porch where they could watch the sun break over the horizon. A young starling was chirping on a stepping-stone. It seemed to have fallen from its nest trying to fly. It occurred to Eve she'd never seen the corpse of a bird that died from old age.

"Where do birds go to die?" she said to her husband, to the shimmers of early daylight flickering on her toes.

"I was just wondering the same thing myself," she heard him say. He put down his coffee and put his arms around her. She felt ready then, for anything; it only took a lifetime. She could let go of him, of her own corporeal self, toward that inevitable, eternal sleep. It was impossible to be without him, however much she tried. He would always be there in every step, every blink, every breath.

She turned to clutch at the shape of him, but her hand fell at the emptiness, threads of air passing between her fingers. He had died before her after all, despite his insistence. At the funeral, she had honored his wishes and in front of their friends, their friends' children and grandchildren, she'd said, *He loved me. He loved me well.*

She looked at the coffee mug now half filled with rain on the lawn table, the last he'd drunk from, his lip imprints still on the cup's rim. He'd fallen asleep in the armchair reading their Italy journal, one of the many travelogues they kept. *He worked hard. He deserves a long, dreamless sleep*, she thought. Alone with the nestling bird, she laughed quietly to herself. *Oh hush, leave me alone. I should join you soon enough.*

Even after all these years, having seen more than a thousand sunrises, it seemed no matter how attentively Eve watched the gradients on the horizon, she couldn't pinpoint the moment vermillion coalesced into blue.

Eve strained her memory for her husband's words, his last. He had only been trying to tell her about the weather, to convince her to go for a walk, yet the truth of his words now brought tears to her eyes.

It's as beautiful as it feels, I promise.

It was so.

THE VOID OF
CARDS

I n the deepest blue, Eve wakes.

She comes like the others, as ashes, as dust, gray specks of nothing that used to be whole cities, the heart of a whale, a girl's eyelash. Here are the memories of her life, the whole of her past, infinite possibilities of lives she did not live, puzzles she did not solve—reeling in a storm of dust. Her consciousness blinks in and out of existence so that she is sometimes a great oak tree, a fly, then suddenly she is a sound, the music of growing grass.

She is never the same thing twice there, where oceanic waves of sand drift and whirl without wind. She's fallen into the sky. She is everything all at once, which is to say, she is finally as she should be, as everything that exists and ceases to exist, returned and reduced to the vast empty. The nothing and nothing that goes on endlessly.

She is the son she never had, the son she did have. She is the blue of veins, the red of blood. She is her enemies and their beloved. She is the man she loved and the woman she failed to love. The cards settle: the ultimate destination.

She arrives.

ACKNOWLEDGMENTS

I am partial to all things second—second chance, second child, second place, second try, which allow for renewal, possibilities, not doing things perfectly the first time. *Constellations of Eve* is not my first book. It is thoroughly second in its construction, in its skeleton and soul, in its being born at the first major crossroad in my relationship with my husband.

My Buddhist upbringing has taught me that things return and return, objects, people, lives, feelings. Unresolved grief could come back in the form of a child, a phantom, weather. The natural world converges seamlessly across time and space. Since I was a girl, I've been looking for signs of my father, his reincarnation. What would my life be like had he lived? Where would our family be? In another universe, perhaps, that version is playing out—my father lives; my mother is not alone. Somewhere, in yet another reality, my husband and I do not make it past our ordeal. Somewhere, we separate. I'm grateful to the kinder traditional Buddhist belief in the after, the second. *Constellations of Eve* was written in this spirit.

I owe a lot to the women in my life, Ngô Vũ Minh Châu, Lina Li, Lucinda Knaus, Caroline Bodian, Melanie Shaw, who understand imperfect relationships and who have provided me with their compassionate support in many forms. They are my second and chosen family. I am grateful to my sister, Ash Mayfair, who never takes more than one day to read my work, whether it is a short story or a novel, for her confidence in this book; and to my younger sibling Arden, whose wisdom is well beyond her years and continues to astound me. Thank you to my mother Đặng Thị

Hoàng Yến, who said, "What is yours, is yours," to remind me that some things are known only by the stars.

I'm lucky to have William Boggess as a trusted reader. His unfailing honesty, technical eye, and moral support are what every writer needs. I'm sorry he'll have to read more stuff from me. I'm also grateful to Jessica Sticklor for being an early reader and advocate.

I am continually indebted to my agent Stacy Testa for her constant belief in me and my work, her many words of reassurance, calm, and support over the years, her shared sorrow when I flounder, her mutual joy when I succeed, and her humor when I don't quite manage to be an adult. Thank you, Stacy.

My deepest thanks to the Diasporic Vietnamese Artists Network, to the founders Isabelle Thuy Pelaud and Viet Thanh Nguyen, and to their editorial board who have given my work a chance when I thought no chance existed. I'm grateful to the entire team at Texas Tech University Press for their partnership and their author-driven approach in publishing. My editor Travis Snyder makes me feel like the luckiest author in the world. His analysis and understanding of my work are more breathtaking than the work itself. I'm thankful for his creative collaboration, observations and insights, his generosity that extends beyond the book, his friendship. Thank you, Travis. This book is also in the skillful hands of my publicist Beth Parker, a tireless advocate and a tenacious voice in the industry, for which I am grateful.

As ever, I am lucky have Tristan Shands to accompany me through life. From his love I draw the strength to create. Thank you for being there through countless hours of my whining, for soothing my fears and anxiety, and for always reading despite how hard it may be. The line in the novel, *the only thing I want on my obituary is that I've loved you—I've loved you well*, is his.

ABOUT THE AUTHOR

Abbigail Nguyen Rosewood is a Vietnamese and American author. Her first novel, *If I Had Two Lives*, is out from Europa Editions. Her short fiction and essays can be found at Salon, Lit Hub, Catapult, and *BOMB*, among other venues. She is the founder of the immersive art and literary exhibit Neon Door. She lives in New York with her husband, their three cats, and a dog.